Others by April Campbell

Mind Games
My Enchanted Hideaway
Dark Side of Destiny

Short Story
in
From The Shadows:
A Dark Secret

Sweet but Psycho

April D. Campbell

authorHOUSE

AuthorHouse™
1663 Liberty Drive
Bloomington, IN 47403
www.authorhouse.com
Phone: 1 (800) 839-8640

Published by AuthorHouse 03/10/2020

ISBN: 978-1-7283-5078-3 (sc)
ISBN: 978-1-7283-5077-6 (e)

Print information available on the last page.

Any people depicted in stock imagery provided by Getty Images are models, and such images are being used for illustrative purposes only. Certain stock imagery © Getty Images.

This book is printed on acid-free paper.

Because of the dynamic nature of the Internet, any web addresses or links contained in this book may have changed since publication and may no longer be valid. The views expressed in this work are solely those of the author and do not necessarily reflect the views of the publisher, and the publisher hereby disclaims any responsibility for them.

This is a work of fiction. All of the characters, names, incidents, organizations, and dialogue in this novel are either the products of the author's imagination or are used fictitiously.

Dedication

GOD

To My Wonderful Family

My awesome best friends Micheal Brewer and David Campbell. Kevin, Luke, my wonderful grandmom Georgeanne Grey, my crazy sisters Tiffany and Juanita, Agnes Parrot, Aurelious Jones, Jr., Terrence Saysay, Tamir Linder, Carmela and Cori Pascarella, Taleba Gee, Lena Mayer-Coleman, Keisha Perry-Bradford, Arkenny Moore, Tish Smith, Shanay Garrett, Meghan Lyons, Michele Bell-Foss, and Michael Veselsky

"I love you all, y'all are my greatest supporters/fans and y'all mean the world to me!!!!!"

Special Dedication

To my son David

I'm super proud of you! I've watched
you grow into a young man who is very
responsible and has a great head on your
shoulders. Keep up the hard work and
don't let anyone tell you that you can't do
something when you know you can! You
gave me hope when others have failed me.
I gave you such a strong name because I
believe that you will become more than
your name. You are truly are a blessing.

To Dear Kevin

I may not have gave birth to you but I loved
as my own. I thank God for allowing me
to be your "step mom" or mom who want

some. I can never replace what you lost but I damn sure that I am proud of the man you have become. Fuck anyone who has a problem with me being your step mom.

To my youngest baby boy, Luke

I am very proud of you. I know that I did the best for you. I can say I am so proud what you did when were 13. No one can replace or take away that you are blood. You born from the rarest diamond God has created. Remember where you came from because NO ONE can take that from you! I will always love you no matter what path you take.

I am proud to call y'all my boys and I'm proud to be your mother. Each one of you have saved my life in many way more than once.

I love y'all!

"Remember you can always forgive, but it happened, fuck it, and move the fuck forward.

~ David ~

In Loving Memory

In loving memories of those who were dear to me. They will greatly miss but always in our thoughts and memories.

Evelyn Elena Campbell, Willie Freeman, Aurelious Jones Sr., Agnes Louise Warren-Jones, Geraldine Howard, Courtenay Matthews, Anita Howard, Bernd Michael Veselsky, Alicia Davis, Cheryl Stevenson, Saundra Ann Gregory, Mildred Mushinski, Leon Calhou, Dianne Marie Barrar, Tommy "TL" Dickerson, Sean Parrott, Dentra Elizabeth, Deloris Walker, Dorothy A. Matthews, Marquise Matthews, Marquise Green, Eleanor Gerlock, Bertha Williams, Josef Ceralde, Mildred Lee Moore, Denise Boyer-Fasel, Deloris Munson, Holly Kern, and Gladys Robinson

Yesterday, upon the stair,
I met a man who wasn't there.
He wasn't there again today,
I wish, I wish he'd go away.

"Antigonish" (1899)

Chapter One

2012

Here we go again fighting, what the fuck we are doing here. I have no damn idea. It just seems like that is all we know how to do any more. Screaming at the top of my lungs I yelled at him as I pushed him back into the wall. "Hit me! I dare you too, you fucking pussy! I wish you would try to fucking hit me! Is that what gets you hard at night fucking hitting women? He just stared at me with his dark evil eyes, piercing right into me.

He fell hard into the wall. It turned into a

screaming match within twenty minutes of the arguing, he swung back his fist and cold cocked me in my jaw. Oh my fucking god, it felt like I was hit with a bag of bricks. I wanted to drop to the floor and cry, but I was taught to take a punch.

Everything went black for a hot second and there in the kitchen stood my boys with a surprise look in their eyes. You could see the rage building up in my oldest boy Draven. Within seconds, I black out and I really don't remember the rest.

Later that Day

Sorry, my name is Aaliyah Churchill. I am now thirty-three year old African American woman. I have long black hair with blue streaks in it. My eyes are dark brown that has a sense of innocence in it. My lips are full with a slightly rosy colored. I am a medium muscular body with the measurements of 36-38-44 and standing at 5'3. I have legs that run for miles. Therefore, as you see I am an attractive woman. These days I don't feel like myself.

I am a typical girl in all other perspectives, but deep within me, no one really knows me. Not even my boyfriend and closest friends. Something is seriously wrong with me, I need some sense of control and understanding of what is going in my head.

Lately, the voices in my head they sound like rattling and chitter-chatter of people whispering in my head. When I'm lying in my bed, the voices echo from underneath the floor. I can't take it anymore, my head hurts battling these voices never knowing, what they are saying. It is getting harder each day to block them out. I did not hear the voices aurally.

They were much more intimate than that, and inescapable. It was hard to describe how I could hear a voice that wasn't auditory; but the words the voices used and the emotions they contained of hatred and disgust were completely clear, distinct, and unmistakable at times, maybe even more so than if I had heard them aurally. At times I could be walking the street and see people on fire, or maggots oozing out of their eyes.

I waked up in finding myself lying in an alley on a cardboard box. The alley was cold and dark. I lay curled up next to the outside wall of a building. I peered out; I could barely open my eyes. My left eye was hurting like a motherfucker. I had no idea how I ended up in the alley in the first place. I sat up and leaned against the wall. I pushed my long dark hair out of my eyes. Laying my head back, I muttered to myself, "Not again." Something is seriously fucking wrong with me.

After a few deep breaths, I stood up and scanned my body for any more injuries. Lucky for me, this time I won't have to make an emergency trip to the hospital. I knew the staff at the local emergency room, I always caught them rolled their eyes when they had to treat me. Self-inflicted wounds they like to called it. Bullshit!

I have found myself going in the same places again and again only to be asked, "Did you forget something?" by the local store owners or bars or, "Why are you pacing up and down the street?" I need fucking help but I was scared to find out.

I have been greeted on the streets by people

who were strangers to me, but call me by different names. I didn't dare to ask why they called me a different names. I just said hello and kept it moving. It would have felt awkward to explain to them why I can't remember them, so I just say I experience amnesia, which is true, but not completely detailed.

I sometimes wake up with bruised up and down my body. There were pictures and videos on my phone. I couldn't recall taking even if I tried, but to tell me a story what may have happened. Sometimes, I was lucky to find my phone. There are so many times, I find myself waking up in strange places never knowing how I got there.

At times, I find blood on my hands. While glimpse of a horror movie plays over and over my head. I don't know whether it's from a movie or I'm actually seeing things. I started noticing unusual things happening around me.

First, a sense of disconnection with reality, for instance, I did not have memories of incidents, but rather felt I had second-hand knowledge of things. I lost a sense of wholeness and this is the hardest thing to explain. Later, I would find bags of shopping with items I, as me, would have never have bought, such as sexual bondage, clothing, etc.

When I visit the hospital, they wanted to send me Emerald Grove Mental Institution Hospital down in Winslow, NJ. This institution offers a multidisciplinary team approach to development and implementation of care, which I think is full of shit. Emerald is one of New Jersey's largest public psychiatric hospitals. They could kiss my ass if they thought I was going there.

Stupid bastards! What the hell, did they know? I was trying to avoid being committed because I could never remember why I had bruises and cuts all over my body at times, I agreed to therapy with Dr. Gil Howard, a therapist who specialized in helping people who had a lost memory and trauma in one's life.

The first two sessions consisted of me being frustrated silence as Gil tried to get me to open up. However, I wasn't budging. I walked to the end of the alley, scanning the street for a familiar sign of my location. A wave of relief washed over me as I realized I was only a few blocks from home. "Didn't go far this time, did you."

"It wasn't necessary," the voice answered.

I sighed. I refused to listen to the voices in

my head. I was also relieved I wouldn't have to depend on some long distance transportation to get back home. I took my time walking home, knowing what would be waiting for me there.

"Where the hell have you been?" Scott's voice boomed out as I walked in the door. I simply rolled my eyes at my boyfriend. At least this one stuck around for a few years. The others were always long gone by now, but that is another story.

Don't fucking start with me Scott!" I walked past him and into the small apartment kitchen. I stood at the sink trying to fill a glass of water, my hands were shaking from a lack of sugar, I unfocused my eyes, staring blankly out the window. Scott reached around me and turned off the water. He took the glass from my trembling hand and turned me around, he then pulled me into his chest.

"I'm trying to understand all this," he whispered, "but how am I supposed to keep an eye on you 24/7 when you blank out?"

"It's not your job to take care of me!" Violently, I shoved him back, knocking him against the edge of the counter. "Keep your hands off me!" Nearing hysterics, I paced the small space of the kitchen. Back and forth.... back and forth....pulling at my hair. All I wanted to do was run. Escape.

Scott kept his distance. He knew how to read my moods now. At times, he acted like a fucking idiot quick to jump on me. Of course, I can dish back as well I can give it. In the few years, we have been together; he'd learned to deal with my ever changing mood swings. My emotional reactions to him were like a never-ending roller coaster ride. The constant ups and downs, and twists and turns had him feeling loopy and off balanced, but he was hanging in there.

There was something about me. Something he'd never felt before with anyone else and he wasn't going to walk away, leaving me alone and isolated as all the other people in my life had done. No...he was determined to see this through and prove to me he wasn't going anywhere.

When, I slid down the counter and landed in a tearful heap on the floor, he knew it was his time to step in. He lifted me off the floor and held me tight, gently rocking me back and forth. "It's alright baby. I'm here."

My sobs were slowing as he entered the

bedroom. He laid me gently on the bed and curled in beside me. It was barely six in the morning, but he was exhausted due to the lack of sleep the night before. I had run from the apartment sometime after the argument.

He curled into me and tightened his grip on me. I wasn't getting away. Checking to make sure I was asleep, he closed his eyes and attempted to get some rest of his own.

He woke with a start, realizing I was gone. His panic was short lived, as he heard the shower running. He lay back on the bed and waited for me. I dashed from the bathroom like lightning, immediately searching my closet for something to wear. Scott leaned on one elbow and watched me, trying to judge my mood. He decided to take a chance. "You look rushed," he all but whispered.

"Hmmmmm?" I was preoccupied with clothes. Deciding on skinny jeans and tee shirt, I turned, bouncing on one leg as I pulled my jeans on. "Did you say something?"

He smiled as I pulled the tee shirt on, shaking my long wet hair back into place. I shot him a cool look and sat on the bed next to him. "I called Gil this morning. He's giving me an emergency session in half-a-hour. It's time for him to do his fucking job and help me figure this shit out! Then afterwards I am heading into work"

The sad part is that I actually love seeing Dr. Gil Howard. Gil was a very handsome and well-build tall black man. He had the perfect brown skin, not too dark and not too light either. Oh, my god and chest, his damn shirts were so tight you can see washboard abs. After every session, I made sure I gave him a hug. Listening to his voice was welcoming and fucking sexy.

His voice was a deep as J.C. Carson from *In Living Color* and lips like LL Cool J. All he needed was to say the right words to make my panties wet. The things that ran through my mind, I would jump on that if I were given the chance. He had a jail buzz haircut, green eyes, with a little bit of facial hair and with a great smile. He wasn't married, but he did have a son named DeShawn.

Forty-five minutes later, I was pacing the Gil's office. "What the hell's wrong with me? I don't even remember going out last night!"

"What do you remember?" Gil prompted.

"I remember everything up until the argument. The next thing I know, I'm waking up in a fucking dark alley!" I continued to pace.

"What do you think is going on?"

"I can't explain it.

There are days that I lose track of time. I'm lost. I'm depressed. I have no idea what's going on from one to next. I find myself laughing for no reason at all times. Then, there are days, I wake up in my bed. When I look around, things don't look familiar to me. There be new shit in my room. I don't know where it came from. There's no receipt, no traces of evidence of where it came from. There are days, I wake up crying.

I don't know what's wrong. I can't even figure out what's going on in my head. At times, in my inner thoughts, I can hear voices in the distance whispering. I can barely understand what is being said. It seems to be getting louder lately, overpowering my thoughts until I get a headache and pass out. Sometimes I find myself rubbing my ear lobe and everything it calms down, but it doesn't work as well all the time.

I keep having really bad nightmares. I don't know what they're doing or if they are real. Finding myself in a corner a with just my t-shirts and panties on; sitting in the corner of my room shaking back and forth. I am trembling as images of keep playing over my head. The images are becoming more and more vivid each day. Some days I just want to rip through my skull just to get them to stop.

No matter where I'm at, I randomly start giggling out nowhere. Then I looked at my hands and I see blood everywhere. There is no blood on my hands. It's so funny and then I snap out of it. Almost like something is taking over me and I don't have no control over it. Part of me is fading away and I have no sense of where it's going.

Gil waited for more, but I offered nothing. I just simply paced. Gil stood and walked around to lean on the front corner of his desk. "Would you be open to hypnosis? I can take you back to last night...and all the other times."

I stopped pacing and looked at Gil like he

was giving it serious consideration. "Can you truly do that?"

"It's one of my specialties. I've been doing it for many years."

"Does it work?"

"I'm satisfied with the results it gives, yes. I think you should try it Aaliyah."

I walked to the window and looked out on the crisp fall day. I turned to Gil. "How soon can we start?"

"How about today? There's still enough time. I've blocked two hours for you."

A look of panic swept across my face. I turned back to the window. "Okay...let's get started."

I sat down on the couch. Gil hit a few a switches on the wall and dim the lights I the room. He walked over to desk and sat in a nearby recliner, grab his his notepad. Right before he started he pulled the ball on the cradle. I listen to it as Gil took me through a series of relaxation techniques. It took more than usual due to my agitated state, but eventually, I began to relax.

Gil gave me a few moments of deep breathing before I began to take her back. "I want you to focus on my voice. You are safe and will not be harm in anyway. You will view any memories from a detached perspective. Everything you see, you will view without an emotional attachment. Are you ready?"

I lay silent for a few seconds, and then quietly replied, "Yes."

"See yourself walking down a spiral staircase. You know that at the bottom of this staircase is a door that leads to the memory of why you went out last night and why you went to location you did. You will view this memory without emotional reaction. You will let me know when you've reached the door and are ready to go through it by raising your right index finger."

Gil waited for me to indicate that I was ready. When I did, he continued. "Open the door and walk through it. Tell me what you see."

My body stiffened and my breathing began to quicken. As suddenly as it started, I began to relax again.

"Aaliyah, tell me what you see."

"Aaliyah is resting... I will take it from here."

Gil sat forward in her chair. "Who are you?"

"I am Cicely."

"Cicely, who?"

"I am Aaliyah's inter child. I know all the memories of Aaliyah's childhood."

Gil was no stranger to multiple personality disorder and knew these situations must be handled with great care. "Why does Aaliyah need you?" When, Cicely didn't answer, I have no intention of harming Aaliyah. You have my word." Gil paused, "Are you willing to speak to me?"

"I may....I may not."

Gil decided to push forward. "Why does Aaliyah need you?"

"This is not your concern. It is my job. Now you are talking to Tasha. If you have any questions you can ask me."

"I'm just trying to help Aaliyah. Your cooperation would be beneficial for her. Tasha who are you?" Gil paused again, waiting for Tasha's response. When she received none, she pushed forward again. "Are you the only one who protects Aaliyah?"

"I am the Protector and the bitch you don't

want to piss off, but there are others. We all have our own jobs."

"Who are the others and what are their jobs?"

"I told you this is not your concern! I will not speak to you, it is not my job!"

"Is there another who will speak to me?"

Tasha sighed. My body stiffened again, and then relaxed. She sat up straight in the chair. My eyes opened and locked onto Gil. "I will speak to you."

"Who are you?" Gil prompted.

"I am Jada."

"Who are you Jada?"

"You would not understand who I am."

Gil leaned forward. "Try me."

I shifted in my seat. "I am the mother who is the caregiver of the kids, Aaliyah, and the other souls that are living within Aaliyah. We are different for each individual."

"How so?"

"They are whatever the individual thinks them to be. To Aaliyah, they are friends."

"Can I speak with all the friends?"

Laughter roared out of me.

"Why are laughing?"

"Shit, if you only knew the shit Aaliyah has been through!"

"I would like to know everything."

"I don't you really can."

"Try me, you will be surprised!" Why does Aaliyah need protecting?"

I just smirked at him.

"So she won't be abandoned and hurt again. The Protector helps her survive."

"Why doesn't Aaliyah protect herself?"

"You know nothing of Aaliyah's inner-world."

"Can you tell me?"

"It is not time. But, you will meet them all. We are counting on you. Aaliyah cannot do this alone. It is time for her to heal."

"What does Aaliyah's inner-world consist of?"

"It is more a question of whom, not what, and there are many."

"How many others are there? Can you give me their names?"

"Aaliyah labels them according to their job. There is Tasha the Protector, who is a strong, chauvinistic, disciplined woman. She is VERY protective all the time. The problem with Tasha is the one has all the hate in her. She hates with a passion and can't stand to see another of us hate.

Cicely, the damage child, but she nurturing, warm, peaceful, peace-keeping, spiritual and very loving, but at times she is depressive, not often out. She wears black and hides and suffers all the time. She is very innocent, but not stupid. Cicely, with a lot of Aaliyah's childhood memories.

Josephine, the sex addict and stripper who is a very audacious, self-confident, flamboyant and sexy woman. Many things can trigger for Josephine to come out. She is, somehow, all Aaliyah ever wanted to be or do but never dared to. Don't let her fool you under all her exquisite personality, there is a lot of pain.

And of course, myself and the mother and co-protector. Each has their own job, according to what Aaliyah's needs. It is better to think of them as personalities. We each think, talk, and act very differently from each other. You will make better headway with this type of thinking."

"So you're saying her alters are simply her own personalities to situations in her life?"

"For Aaliyah, this is true, yes?"

"Can you explain about them?"

"There are many emotions that live with in every individual of Aaliyah. Let me ask you this......When you are sad and then you become happy again, have you not become a different person emotionally? When you are angry, you are not the same person you are, as say, when you are depressed"

"I see. This puts a different spin on it."

"Maybe it is time for a....different spin as you call it."

"Can I speak to the other..... personalities?"

"Yes, but I hope you can handle us."

"I will do my best to keep up. I want what's best for Aaliyah."

"Of course."

"Then help me help her. That is my job as well."

"She pays no attention to what we do when we are called on. Aaliyah really can't talk much about her life as well as we can. Mind you, Aaliyah is the main person, but as we mentioned there are more than just one person in her life. We are to simply do our jobs. To be honest, I really do how strong Aaliyah will be, if she had to face all the memories we have suppressed from her.

The best we can get this started is to start from the beginning. By me starting from the beginning of my childhood, I can tell you it wasn't all peaches and cream. Trust and believe me, I wish I could tell you a fairy tale story, but it wasn't all about that.

Boy, do we have lots of memories and crazy stories to tell you! This is your first and last warning Aaliyah is bat shit crazy. I stopped and looked at the doctor and gave him a sinister laugh. You could tell he was bother by the laugh. That he just pushed his chair back further away from me.

Chapter Two

Bamberg, South Carolina

My body stiffened again, and then relaxed. I crawled up into comfortable position on my side facing Gil.

"Hello", I said in a childlike voice.

"Whom am I speaking to?"

"Doctor it's Cicely!"

"Oh hey, how are you?"

"I am good."

"How old are you?"

"I am seven… I am always seven."

"Why you say that?"

"Because Aaliyah."

"Why?"

"Because she doesn't know how to play with the boys like I do and just some memories she has a hard time deal with I dealt with."

"And how's that?"

"Like as kid silly, she doesn't how to be a kid. Plus mommy Jada and Auntie Tasha don't want her knowing what happened."

"When did you come into Aaliyah's life?"

"It was about time my parents started to have problems."

"So Cicely, tell me about your childhood."

"Okay."

Aaliyah's Family

I have two younger brothers Jacques and Terrell. We don't hear much nowadays. My brothers were very young when our world changed. Things were never the same.

Jacques was a tall skinny, wiry child. He only stood a foot and a half shorter than me. He was the middle child. No one really likes talking to Jacques, because the attitude he presents. It was just the fact that if you didn't know him, he didn't get two shits about you.

I loved Jacques. He was 100 with things. But Jacques was also self-centered bastard. Half of the time when I tried to get his attention or try to hang out with him, he didn't have the time for me. It was all about him or nobody else.

Heaven forbid he had one of his well-known tantrums. He was all over the place screaming and yelling. He undergo went a psychiatric evaluation only to find out that Jacques was bipolar. He was diagnosed when he was 6. He was a short fuse some days and other days he was the best person in the world. He had usual and strange behaviors that were not appropriate. He could be unnaturally moody, aggressive, euphoric, or mild-tempered.

Fluctuations in mood from time to time are normal. He would seem like he was "off line" during full blown manic and psychotic episodes, which affect his memory. He could barely recall what happened each time.

I remember, when we were at a family reunion my great grandparent's estate, he was 8 at the time. He chased the neighborhood kid with a pitch fork. Almost had the kid if wasn't for my aunt stopping him.

When Jacques was 11, he was playing on a swing set and was hit in the head with one of the swings. The accident caused a blood clot in his brain, the damage was not discovered until he was 16. Between the time of the accident and the diagnosis, Jacques suffered from blackouts that were caused by the clot.

Now, Terrell was the odd one. He had a learning disability. Terrell had a difficult with reading and writing, problems with math skills, problems paying attention, trouble following directions, poor coordination, difficult with concepts related to time, and problems staying organized. He had hard time remembering things He always seemed to be up to something with his mysterious way. Terrell was the one I had to watch. I have never known what he was up too.

He was in his own little world at times. We can never figure out what he was thinking or doing. The ignorant neighborhood kids always made fun of him. Just like Jacques, he has been nasty he was a mean son of a bitch.

He was a tough person. He was good for pulling and throwing knives at us or pulling my hair. I was afraid of Terrell. I was awakening to him standing over me with a knife. One night I was tied to the bed and he was forcing his dick down my throat. I never told my cousins and grandmom because I knew they wouldn't do shit about it.

He always had a blank look on his face as if no one was home in his head. I want to bite his dick off, but I didn't do it because he was my brother. He was my blood. My brother would do this once in a while over the next few years before getting kicked out.

It got to the point that he would fondle my breasts. I just pretended that I was asleep and let him do what he want to do cuz I know nothing was going happen to stop him from doing so.

The last memory of my dad was when I was little. I could do no wrong. I was daddy's little girl. Dad always held my hand everywhere went go. I would steal his favorite pimp hat. I remember seeing my mother and father always happy especially when we were out and about. He always rock his special hat. He would never go anywhere without this one black hat.

My dad use to play weird games with me like pretending that he had boogers in his hands. He would tell me to give them to my mother. My mother just went along with the joke, hints the nickname *Boogers*.

When, my dad would come home from work I would jump in his arms. Despite after a long day at work he would always walk in with a smile when he saw his family. I was always happy and excited to see my dad.

I remember how my dad love to drink his gin straight up from the bottle. He never drinks from a glass to have his gin. I always finished his bottle with a smile on his face. My dad always taught me to be strong and to never let anyone take my joy. He had given me such security that no one could replace. No matter what mistakes I made he was there for me. We looked happy as family. I never saw my parents fight.

The last day I saw my father, my mother had pancakes for us. There was a knock on the door.

My mom went to the door to answer it. It was the police.

"How may I help you?

"Good morning, we have an arrest warrant for William Otis Franklin. They were there for my dad. My dad was a tall and large dark skinned black man, who was often coming off as intimidating and frightening. But to me he always seemed to be a giant teddy bear in my eyes.

He wasn't a fool. He was the type of man the neighborhood knew not to fuck with. I love how my father had a machete and knives hiding all over the house or on him.

My dad stood up from the table and gave my brothers a hug and kiss. My dad was a tall, stocky man. Trying to give him hug was like climbing a mountain. The police came and pushed my mother aside. My dad looked pissed but he played it cool.

My dad was bending down to ruffle my hair and I sprang up crossing my arms around his neck. "I love you daddy!" I whispered in his ear.

My mom pulled me off my dad as I heard him, saying, "I'll miss you, sweetheart. Be good for your mom and I will see you soon. Please help your mother with your boys. Remember, daddy always loves you! Baby girl, don't cry!"

My dad's love was unconditional and it wouldn't never go away, no matter he was in my life. He had his head up high. I still remember the expression on his face.

He had a strong expression his face. My dad would show his true emotions, but I could see the anguish in his eyes. I did everything I could to hold back the tears in my eyes. I had to be strong for my mother and boys. I didn't want to show a bit of weakness.

Then, I watched as the cops led him out of the house and into the cop car. That was the last time I have seen him. He cure my disappointments and healed my pain but I knew he wasn't going to be able to fix the pain I was feeling.

He was our protector but he was gone. I treasure every irreplaceable memory. No one else will replace my daddy. That night my brothers and I stayed in my parent's room.

I looked out the window of my parent's room. The sky was tar-black and the huge clouds were moving towards me. I could hear a tapping on the window and then it became a pitter-patter. Puddles began plunking as the rainfall became heavier. The roof of house danced with each spray of rain. I could hear the murmuring of the rain through the window. It sounded like the buzzing of angry flies.

As it continue rain outside, all I could do was brushing my mother's hair as she cried herself to sleep. Once every one was asleep, the tears poured out. I couldn't stop the tears from falling. I just knew he wasn't coming back. After that night I would get emotional thinking about my father. I refuse to show any tears or pain. Tough girl I had to be.

My mother was a thin, but tall African American woman. She was born Philadelphia, PA. She wasn't as strict as her mother. She beautiful person inside and out, but that were slowly disappearing. She was having a hard time dealing with us and with dad she was losing it.

She had a beautiful milk chocolate skin, straight hair neatly coiffed to reveal a chiseled, anguished face. Bloodshot black eyes, set a-symmetrically within their sockets, watch vigilantly over the river they've come to love for so long.

Her smooth skin gorgeously compliments her hair and leaves a pleasurable memory of her fortunate upbringing. She had the face of a beautiful Egyptian Goddess. She stood common among others, despite her light frame. There's something inexplicable about her, perhaps it's her good will or perhaps it's simply her personality. But nonetheless, people tend to shower her with gifts, while hoping to one day follow in her footsteps

Once my father was gone, my mother became ill. She was always fighting with my grandmom. There were days she wouldn't come home. When she was home, she was sleeping. Then just like my father, she disappeared.

Chapter Three

Mount Orleans, NJ

Now, we had to move in with my twin cousins Delilah and Phyllisa who were toxic people. This was in Mount Orleans, New Jersey. They lived in the Gardens, which was the projects. We left everything behind, in South Carolina. The country life we once knew was just a faded memory. We knew the love that we got from our parent was all a memory. We knew that we surrounded by a family that didn't show affection. I knew I was loved, but it was rarely expressed, either in words or with a by hug.

The Gardens were a low-salary neighborhood in the Township of Mount Orleans, New Jersey. African American and Hispanic inhabitants made up the greater part of the tenants of the area's 329 homes. The issues identifying with swarming, empty properties, and wrongdoing have since quite a while ago tormented the Gardens.

We had to visit my grandma on the weekends because they didn't want to be bothered with us. I spent a lot of my childhood attending church with my grandmom, who was a minister. Her touch was so cold at times. I wonder if she even had a soul. Other than that, I loved visiting her.

Delilah was a fucking giant she stood 6'5" and was a good 450lbs. She was bald and wore wigs to cover up her ugly misshaped head. Delilah had her only daughter Jackie at 14 and had to learn to be a parent on her own. Jackie was older than I was. She ended moving in with Phyllisa, when she was 18.

Jackie was the main center of attention. Everyone praised her. My cousin thought she was perfect. Physical attributes made other girls envious and boys drool. Don't ask her to talk, because being dumbass as doorknob. Bitch dropped out high school in her junior year in high school. "DUMB THIRTSY HOE" should be tattooed on her head.

She always was chasing after guys you were being a rising star in some kind of sport. She would be three different guys each week. If the guy didn't do what she wanted, she then would break up with them, then move to the guy. Jackie had shoulder length brown hair with fake ass hazel brown eyes.

She was tall with full hips and over size tits; of course the boys loved her. If they are actually seen how dirty this bitch lived, they probably take bleach baths. Her pussy was like seven eleven, opened 24/7 with every dick slinging inside out. I am surprised the bitch knows who the father is to her first-born. Jackie has been just like her fucking mother Delilah.

Now Phyllisa, I never really did like her. We were forced to live with her unfortunately. She owned a dog which was the only thing I liked. He was a German shepherd and was part wolf. I would play with the dog more thing anything, when I was forced to go outside. Until she left to me to care of him, then he was pain in the ass.

Phyllis was very interesting. She went to college. She got her degree in Business. She never went any further than that. She worked about 2 to 3 different jobs at one time. So, we barely seen her. When, we did see her it was beat our ass or be told to do something within her house wasn't done to her damn liking. She was a lazy piece of shit. She always had time to sit on her ass and entertained some new dick each weekend.

I remember one night waking up in the middle night to moans, groans, and screaming I thinking that one of my relatives got hurt so I snuck off my bed and cruise down to the hallway and her door was ajar I opened it up a little bit more on the find her spread eagle underneath of gentleman.

I asked her next morning who it was and she quote that was "the doctor". I later found out it was just another man, she was fucking. She was lazy most of the time, she would asked us to come in her room to handle something that was only within walking distance of her bed or she would ask us to take pictures of her lingerie. It was really creepy at the age of 10 taking pictures of your cousin spread out in different sexual positions and in lingerie.

Knowing damn well that the lingerie didn't fit. We didn't do as we were told. We would get hell from her. We would get beat with everything and anything that she can get her hands on. We could since that she hated us. Especially by the smart comments that she made with Delilah about my brothers and me. It was so uncomfortable at times, but we did what we did and had to listen as best as we could or between Delilah and Phyllis are punishment would have been worse than the last punishment. Punishment by my cousin did get worse. She used to have us going down into the basement stand against the wall with our hands up on it. With our backs facing, we had stay in that position while she beat us with a wooden cane until we drop to the floor.

Phyllisa was scary to be around with. Just hearing her footsteps pitter-pattering on the hardwood floors of the house just made you run. Phyllisa just finished college and didn't have any kids. She was cold as ice. When she tried to play with us, she just yelled at us.

We could never tell if she was mad or just fucking loud. Most of time, she was in rare form, she put our heads between her legs, locking her ankles so we couldn't break free, and then put a blanket over our heads. It was scary and she thought it was funny.

My grandmom was born in Philadelphia and definitely had the Philly attitude. My grandmom was strict, but she loved us. My grandma was a sweet person. She was a homemaker. She spent most of the time at home or working with the church in the local neighborhood. It was always a pleasure to go over her house.

She was a beautiful tall curvy woman but she wore clothes so neat no matter how long she's been cleaning the house or how dirty things were around her, she always seem to be spotless. I would take a white glove across her clothes after she's been cleaning and when she was messing in the garden. She was always spotless.

I could never understand her. She was always giving us the biggest hugs and the longest ones. I always felt welcome and loved. It's a big difference from living with the other two.

My grandmom who was the maid and the cook at her house in Philadelphia. Grandmom was in middle of a divorce from her second husband, which was an asshole. I remember a time we were watching *Sesame Street* and he wanted to be a jerk. He kept unplugging the TV. My grandma warned him to leave we allow. But by the third time of yelling at him.

They were fighting. He kept hitting her and was punching him back. The fight continues into the bedroom where we were, they ended in the bedroom. Before I knew it, my grandmom broke a crystal bowl over his head.

She walked out of the bathroom, straight into the kitchen and finished washing dishes. My grandpop came out of bathroom falling all over place with blood pouring out of his head. That's what the bastard gets! He never bothers ever again.

There were planning of my grandmom

moving in with us. This was going to interesting because there were too many people as it was.

Growing up in my house wasn't preaches and creams. Living in a house with all women was not my idea of fun! A bunch of women bitching about everything and anything was so damn annoying.

I swear there is something seriously wrong with this family. I really don't understand why they even agree to take care of us. They don't even love us. They damn sure don't act like parents are even family. This dysfunctional family was no different than any other family with a lot more skeletons.

My cousins don't even pay any attention to my brothers and me. Most of the time the days just passed. I don't remember half time I try to stay in my room and stay the hell away from everyone. Aaliyah keeps me busy; she is the person I trust.

My grandmom would come over to watch us from time to time, but lately we have been going over to my great grandmom's house more. We started to go to her house more and more each month when school was out. My cousin Evan lived there. I didn't like to go over my great grandmom's when he was around. He was too touchy.

Entertaining in my house was movies and occasionally cooking when the entire family gather Grandmom came over and made dinner apparently Phyllisa and Delilah needed to talk to us. It was never good when all of us had to sit down for dinner.

It was time for dinner when my grandmom yelled up the stairs. Jackie came running out of the room just as I was about to walk down the stairs. This evil bitch as pushed my brothers and me out of the way, so she could get to the table first, greedy bitch. I came down the stairs behind Jackie can see suitcases by the front door.

"Come on Aaliyah, Jacques, and Terrell time to eat." My grandma said as she stood in the kitchen doorway.

"Why are there suitcases by the door?"

"Sit down and we tell you about it." Phyllis said as she started filling her plate up with food.

"Okay," I sat down next to my brothers.

"Well the news is that y'all are going over your great grandmom's for the summer. Is Jackie going too?"

Jackie laughed," Just you and your fucking brothers!" I am staying here. My mom and cousin Phyllis are sending just y'all over there, because they don't want to deal with y'all this summer. You guys are fucking pain in the ass!"

Before, she could get another word out of her fat mouth, my grandmom popped her one in her mouth with a wooden spoon. The look on her face was priceless. A moment I will never forget. I loved it!

I wanted to laugh, but I knew better. Terrell and Jacques were happy, but I wasn't. "Is Cousin Evan going to be?"

Probably, why you asked?"

He makes feel uncomfortable."

"Girl it's all in your head. Stop it you are going there and that's that!"

The next morning we headed to my great grandmom's. There in the yard was my cousin.

Chapter Four

Cousin Evan

My cousin Evan was a big fat man who was a mouth breather. He was really creepy at times. Evan had that one crazy eye that just kept wandering left and right and never stopping. I learned later it was a condition called, Nystagmus, which is the involuntary movement of the eye.

He also had a clubfoot that sometimes he dragged behind him when he didn't have his special shoes on. He looked like something out of a horror movie. Evan was always lurking in every corner of the house no matter where I was, he was there. I had no idea, but it really made me uncomfortable.

I use to love going to my great grandmom's house except when my cousin Evan was there. It was three-bedroom ranch that was out in the country of the back part are of Mount Saint-Paul, New Jersey.

I used to love going to my grandma's house she had a beautiful house a Rancher. The closest house was right next door which was my great grandfather's house was. My great-grandfather and great-grandma we're still married but didn't live under the same roof. I never questioned it, but I always love going to visit my grandparents' house.

When, grandfather died, the house next door stayed empty. The grass grown yay high. The family didn't give a shit about it, either. I can't remember the last time I was in it. My grandma used to exchange fruits and vegetables with the local neighbors who had a farms.

We would go to the local police department

for water. She had well water so it was better to get the water from the police department. We would fill up gallons of water.

I always love going over my great-grandma and helping her with things it was nice and peaceful away from where I had to deal with at my damn cousins. My brothers seem to be better-behaved there. They didn't try all the weird foolish things at great grandmom's. It was nice! Aaliyah was good and I didn't have to come out much but there were times I will come out just to play and enjoy being a kid.

Trouble

The night everything changes. Aaliyah was waked up in the middle of the night to go to the bathroom. She was hoping that if she walked quietly by her cousin's door to the bedroom, she won't wake him up.

She went into the bathroom, closed the door softly behind her, and sat down on the toilet, she started to pee, when a she started rubbing her left ear, then the next minute I know I was there.

Aaliyah had a bad feeling a bad feeling didn't want to deal with would happen next.

I keep praying to myself that he wouldn't hear me as I finished up and I flushed the toilet. I washed my hands and waited for the toilet to stop running. I turned off the lights and slowly opened the door.

I begin to tiptoe back to the bedroom. I was right in front of my great grandmom's door when I heard his voice, "Who is out there?" I tried to keep walking and act as if I didn't hear him. I was so close to my door when just then he stuck his head out of his door and told me to come here. I turned to him and asked him what do you want?

"Come here and be quiet!"

Knowing how nasty my great grandmom can be when you wake her up. I went to him. I didn't want to give him an excuse to tell Phyllis that I did something I didn't do. He pulled me into his room and closed the door behind him. He told me to lie down on the bed. I lay down and closed my eyes. I could feel his hands rub up my legs.

He reached up my night gown and pulled it up over my waist. He kept telling me to relax.

I didn't want to relax I wanted to go to bed. He pulled my panties down and spread open my legs. He was rubbing his hands on my private parts. I kept my eyes close I didn't want to see what he was doing. I was hoping that this was a bad dream.

About thirty minutes, later he told me to pull up my panties and told me to go to bed. Before I left the room, he grabbed by my arm and whispered in my ear that "This was our little secret and not to tell anyone. If you do tell I will hurt your brothers and tell your mother how are so bad when you are over here. Remember baby girl doesn't tell anyone or I will hurt you as well and I won't be gentle"

I just nodded, shaking, crying, and hugging myself because I felt lost and confused about what just happened. Knowing how afraid I was of my grandmom and cousins, I was too scared to tell anyone what had happened. This happened every time we came over my great grandmom's.

My grandmom was not aware of it at all. Aaliyah would close her eyes each them. Every day and every night, he would touch me. It became easier for Aaliyah to hide and for me to deal with what was going on.

The HELL

Aaliyah's great grandmom made the biggest mistake of her life this weekend. She left Aaliyah and her brothers allow with him. Aaliyah tried her hardest to go with her. Nevertheless, her grandmom slapped Aaliyah crossed her face and told her to stay.

As Aaliyah watched, her great grandmom left the house in the neighbor's car. Tears filled her eyes for she knew what was coming. Aaliyah was praying and hoping her cousin was going to leave her allow. Just then, her cousin walked into the kitchen and told her to come into his room when she was done eating. A knocked formed in her throat, she was having a hard time swallowing, crying at the same time, so I stepped in, and let Aaliyah go and do her thing.

I picked my head up; got up from the table; put my plate in the sink. With a last look into the kitchen, I stealthily left the living room. I reached the Evan's bedroom and knocked softly. He opened the door and pulled me in.

The bedroom light was turned off. The streetlight shone through the white homemade curtains on the window outlining Evan's bed and student desk. I could hear the TV in the other bedroom as my brothers were playing.

"The way to play this game is you take off your pants, and I take off my pants, okay?" Evan said, his voice breaking on the last word.

I pushed off my overall down, leaving them twisted around my ankles.

"Now we take our undies off," Evan instructed.

I frowned at this new game, I didn't like showing my privates, but the little bit of darkness made me feel secure in tugging my panties down.

The sound of his heavy breathing filled the room. Evan moved closer and stood over me, his hands pressed against the wall on each side of my head. He bent his knees and rubbed his penis between my legs, his breath blowing into my face. He pushed between my legs, making me lean harder against the wall.

He made me kneel down in front of him as

he unzipped his fly and hauled out his erection. "Take it deep, little girl, and use your tongue."

I leaned forward, opened my lips, and allowed my cousin to insert his penis into my moist young mouth. I had never felt so humiliated or degraded in my life, to be kneeling here, sucking off my cousin. I was trying so hard not to cry. I wanted to run away.

After, a couple of minutes of sucking, I felt his penis begin to swell. He clasped his hands on the sides of my head and thrust deeper into my throat. I started to gag, but fought down the urge, as his penis erupted, shooting stream after stream of warm white cream deep into my throat. I swallowed repeatedly until he was done.

He then said," Now that you made me feel good; it's my turn to make you feel good! He we are going to have a bit more fun."

I had no idea what that meant. Next he made lay on the bed. He finished undressing me. He kneeled on the floor in front of me and spread my legs open. He put his hands on my thighs, "You know you are very pretty,"

I shook my head," No." No one has even said

I was pretty, I felt very special since my dad and mom disappearing.

He puts head in between my knees. He put his mouth on me. I could feel him licking and sucking on me. This was something new. I had no idea what I was feeling. Just then, he stopped and got up. He was leaning over me rubbing his penis across my private and before I knew it more white stuff coming out of him on to me.

He lifted me up and gave me a hug as he said," Thank you, you know you make your cousin very happy and I love you! Now it's time take your bath and get ready for bed."

He carried me into the bathroom and begins to run a bath for me.

I sniffle," Can I have bubbles?"

He nods his head while saying, "Remember do not tell anyone about what happened or I'm going to hurt you."

I nodded in fear, "I won't tell anyone."

I really didn't feel like crap anymore because my cousin was happy. I didn't need to be scared. After being at my great grandmom's for the month it was time to go home.

Back Home

Phyllis was not happy to have us back. My grandmom made dinner that night for us and then she sent us to bed early. I was heading to my room when there was a knocked on the door. It was my cousin Evan.

That was odd he never comes over the house. I immediately got scared but excited at the same time. I said hey and headed to bed. About two hours into the night, Evan was in our room asking Terrell to come in the bathroom with him.

That was odd because he always asked me to come with him. I watched as they both went into the bathroom. Two minutes later, I wanted to see what was going on. Evan was getting undress as Terrell was in my pajama dress. Terrell was so small I didn't want him to touch him like he was doing to me. He didn't want to listen to me. No matter what I did, he still didn't want to leave the bathroom.

After, fighting with my brother to come to bed, I left him in there. I ran into my room, jumped in my bed. I pulled the covers over my head and started to cry. I was scared for my brother. I was pissed because he wanted my brother and not me. What did I do wrong? I began to get worried. My grandmom started yelling up the stairs to get to bed.

I guess she realized what was going on and came running up the stairs and find Terrell in the bathroom with my cousin. She flipped out and ordered Terrell to go to bed and for my cousin to leave. She ran behind Evan with a belt in her hand, beating all the way down the stairs.

I acted surprised that Terrell was in the bathroom with my cousin. My cousins and grandmom didn't dare to ask Terrell what had happened, but instead yelled at me for not waking up to help Terrell and that Terrell asked for it. After everything was said and done, they just told us to go to sleep. That night I felt angry for the first time, but I didn't know why.

The next morning my grandmom and Phyllis took us to the doctor to check out. Terrell was good. No signs of being hurt, but for me, he said my skin was broken whatever that meant. I would learn years what that meant. I next saw my cousin again and didn't dare to talk about what happened.

Things between my brother and I was never the same after that night. Nor did we even speak of what had happened.

As the years pass

As the years went by, my cousin Delilah and Phyllisa became even lazier especially, when it came to teaching us things that was important. Instead of teaching about the sex. They made us watch TV specials as if that was going to help.

Therefore, they would teach us all the time with other important things like English and math. Anytime we asked questions about sex we were watching another damn TV special.

I learned about sex from the neighborhood boys and girls. We talked about it on the regular basis. I started to blossoming is when I really found out more about "the birds and the bees". It wasn't the way that a child should learn about it. I learned the simple stuff that from the educational programs but between learning about it and from my friends was disparate. I was now curious I yearned to learn more about sex. I started to tug on my ear around and to stop. Just then I could feel a change in my demeanor.

Aaliyah and Gil

Just then I was Aaliyah was back in charge. I woke up and found myself still on the couch. I sat up and asked, "Gil are you getting anywhere?"

He jumped to my question and replied," Yes, we are and I have decided that we would stay here as long as possible. I got rid of my appointment so, we'll be here for a while. Is there anything you want to eat I will order it? I guess this a perfect time to take a break."

I was taken by what the doctor was doing for me. "You sure cuz I do have to go to work but I can always call out."

"That is fine whatever you feel like doing. I will give you a letter for your job if that would help. If you don't mind, can you please tell me how much you would have lost today if you went into work?"

"Just for the record I was supposed to work 6 hours tonight that's $100 a pop per hour so, that is $600. I would have lost tonight but you're lucky. I just got off the phone with my boss. My boss said that because it's a medical reason why I am not coming in. I wasn't going to lose hours. He was going to give me a check for that for at least half of what I would have lost so you're lucky doctor

Gil choked and manager to speak," Alright fine, I will throw in $300 and session is free. And by the way, it seems like I'm just scratching the surface. Vaguely, I'll be more than happy to order anything that you would like."

"I beginning to think you have a thing for me doctor!" I winked an eye at him. He just grinned back me.

"If you don't mind I would like to make a phone call and let my family know where I'm at, so they don't have any problems. Is there any way you could call *King China* and ordered me a barbecue boneless spare ribs with fried rice and a shrimp egg roll, don't forget a wonton soup…..please. If you don't mind! Thank you!"

"Anything you want Aaliyah that would be great. I order it now! Call your family and we will start back on the session if you're up to it."

"Yeah! I'm up for it!"

I was actually surprised that the doctor didn't want to go home to take a shower and to see his son, but he wanted to stay here and continue the session. I also wanted to get to the bottom of this. I know something's wrong. I just can't do this with some kind of help. I got to get it done. We sat down and ate little bit. Soon afterwards I went back in to a trance.

I commence to tug on my ear again. Just then I could feel my demeanor change.

"Aaliyah, are you there?" The doctor knew it wasn't but he had to ask.

I'm not Aaliyah. I felt so empowered. A warm feeling just ran through my body. I felt so sexy so in control just like I did at work. I knew who Josephine was and I like her but I stayed in the back as she thought I didn't I knew. I let her come out and play but I enjoy watching.

Well the doctor wanted to know everything.

I guess the girls going to come out and play. I don't remember everything but I do remember bits and pieces at times. There are times where I don't I black out completely. This should be fun.

Introduce Josephine

With my best voluptuous voice I leaned over and smiled at the doctor and said, "Well......
hello doctor..... Gil."

The doctor became nervous as he questioned me. "Who am I talking to?"

"You are talking to Josephine and to you its Miss Josephine or at work Miss Spice!"

"Okay, Miss Josephine how are you today?"

"I don't know what kind of game you are playing with Aaliyah and these memories. You are treading in thin water. You will be opening Pandora's Box. I am sure you will not be able to handle what you find out."

"I'm not playing any games. I'm trying to get to the bottom of things and help her but with all the different people living in her head. I don't know who to work with or how the help her. I really need your and everyone else to help. Aaliyah needs to know everything. Josephine, why have you arrived?"

"Okay doctor! Well, as you know going through a lot of things already and it's still early. I am a sexual side, the feisty side of Aaliyah as you well know. I have a huge favor that I need from you before I can go any further."

"Sure anything you need. What's that?"

"I need you to get on all four and eat my pussy like it's the last fucking meal you're ever."

"Excuse me!?"

"I'm pretty sure I didn't fucking stutter! If you want this session to continue. Well, I need for you to eat me."

"I'm not that kind of doctor. I like to keep everything very professional."

"Sure you fucking do! You're telling me right now if I was to get undressed and just laid here and played with myself."

He started to hesitate and I could tell the things start to change in his demeanor. He was licking his lips. He started to sweat as I begin to undress. He adjusted his tie and just looked at me.

"What's wrong doctor, cat got your tongue!

I know that you want this. It's not like Aaliyah will even remember this. Plus she's been dying to have your face planted in her pussy and a nice dick ride.

Therefore, I strongly suggest if you want any information out of me. You need to start taking me more serious. I promise to tell you how I came about. The doctor ended up taking his tie and shirt off. He revealed the sexiest muscular body I have never seen in a while. He came over to the couch and pull down my pants.

"Don't worry doctor, this will be our little secret. Aaliyah doesn't have to know. For the rest of us….. will…. I suggest you do a very…. very good job!"

He took my knees in his hands and spread my legs wider and lifted them over his shoulder, letting my feet rest on his back. My pussy lips parted slightly, as if it where welcoming Gil's attention.

He lean forward, feeling my heat against his face, and smelt my fragrance, sweet and heavy. He started to lick the edges of my lips, up and down, soft and gentle. I moaned and took my breasts in my hands, kneading them and pulling my nipples to help them harden, something that didn't need much help as they quickly became erect and responsive to my touch.

Gil continued to softly lick my labia, making sure not to touch my clitoris with his tongue or enter my pussy at this point. His fingers ran over my stomach and he felt me twitch at his touch. Then he returned to her thighs.

I was still massaging my breasts and pulling on my nipples, pinching them gently and writhing slowly with my hips, trying to get Gil's tongue to run over my clit, but Gil was following my movements and was not going to be easily misled.

My moans started to get louder as Gil's tongue slowly worked its way closer to my clit. He touched it softly with the tip of his tongue and I moaned with pleasure. He started to lick my clitoris, massaging it and running his tongue down and flicking it in and out of my pussy.

My swirling became faster, and I squeezed my nipples harder, pulling on them at the same time. Gil continued to lick me, and every now and again he sucked on my clit, feeling how hard it had become, how wet it all was round my pussy.

Gil brought a hand up to my pussy, licked the fingers, and gently inserted a finger into my vagina, moving it round and in and out slowly. I missed a breath as I felt his finger gliding in, and then groaned as Gil put a second finger in.

Gil was still licking my lips and clit as he explored the inside of my pussy, using the motion of my hips to help heighten the sensation. He curled his fingers up towards the area of my vagina just below my clitoris. Now, he could use his tongue to push down on my clit while, his fingers supported it from inside.

As, Gil licked and massaged my clit, he pushed down on it, feeling the response of my body as it writhed and bounced at his touch.

My breathing was loud and I started to gasp as Gil kept licking and sucking and pushing on her clitoris. He brought his other hand up and took over massaging one of my breasts and nipples.

I put my now free hand on the back of Gil's head and pushed it against my clitoris, increasing the pressure on it as I felt my stomach and pussy muscles start to contract. I brought my legs, which had been resting on Gil's back, up into the air, feeling the tension in my thighs.

Gil rolled the nipple he had between his fingers, licked my clitoris vigorously and finally sucked hard on it. All of my muscles tightened as I arched my back as a pure sensation of Fantasy Show-bar flooded though my body and I held my breath momentarily before exhaling and moaning as I came, and came, and came.

I pushed Gil's head against my pussy, trying to extract every possible bit of orgasm out of my body. At last, Gil felt me relax and sink back against the couch, gasping and trying to catch my breath.

Doctor got up wiped his face and return back to his seat I clean myself up and laid back on the couch with the most devilish grin on my face. I had the doctor where I wanted him eating out of the palm of my hands.

"Why are you even a part of Aaliyah?" he asked as he put back on his shirt.

"Well, you see after the little adventure that Aaliyah had with Maya. It sparked a little sinister interest for sex in Aaliyah. Therefore, I'm the part of Aaliyah that allows her to be sexual and sexy at the same time. Despite the flaws on my body I am totally comfortable in this body.

I am very confident about my own sexiness and all the good things linked to contact with other people. This doesn't necessarily include sex. It's also in eye contact. In a hug or a kiss on the cheek even in a conversation and of course in sex.

"Who is Maya?"

"In due time, you will find out."

"Okay"

"Let's get started.......doctor!"

Chapter Five

Who is Miss Josephine?

"Please Miss Josephine, tell me more about yourself."

"Before I tell you more about me, answer a few questions for me."

"Okay, what would like to know?"

"Why do you want to know so much about me?

"Truthfully, out of everyone, you seemed to be more outspoken."

"It's not that I am outspoken that you like! It's me that you like more than anything."

"Meaning?"

"You may hesitated when I told you to eat me, but there was a desired to do so."

"Yes, ever since Aaliyah walked into my office. I wanted to be with her, but being her doctor causes a conflict of interest. I guess that is all out the window!"

"Exactly!"

"Ever wonder if sex was good or bad? It all depends on how you look at it! My brothers I grew up in a world that doesn't stimulate fun, pleasure or lust. It's encouraged to have a job that consumes most of the time, work hard and to be serious. Sex was a touchy subject. We really didn't talk about it."

"Why are you telling me this?"

"Be patient, Gil. It will all make sense soon!"

"OK, I will shut up and listen!"

"Thank you!"

As, I was saying. My brothers and I were took to pretend that we did not have feelings of lust. We were to pretend that sex was bad. It's a practical thing to do when you get marry and when you and spouse wanted kids, and that was it. I was curious.

At, the same time, I felt guilty for even thinking

about it. Lust was a feeling which was denied. I couldn't trust my emotions. I was starting to go through of changes with my body and mentally.

Changes

The changes I started to go through was of course was puberty. All the sudden my pants were getting too short. The growth spurts were painful in my legs. I was gaining some weight. I felt so awkward it felt like my body was not quite proportional. I was blooming faster than it was expected. Everyone was starting to grow into their own even though I was growing into my own I even start blossom little quicker than I expected my cousin always favored over Terrell. I didn't know why but I find out lately that she was getting more money from the state because he was "special".

My boobs felt they grow over night. I asked my cousin to get me a training bra. Phyllisa just laughed in my face, but she was pissed by the end of the month because she was forced to buy me 34 b bras. I wanted to laugh in her face, but I didn't dare to.

After that my boobs got bigger and fuller, until I stopped at 36 C. I didn't have my cycle yet but I wasn't in a hurry for that to come wasn't looking for dealing with that shit. I think it was waste thing a women have to go to. Little by little, the neighborhood boys were starting to notice. I hear the little the whispers as I would walk by. Aaliyah really didn't feel comfortable but I never really had to step in.

No one I had met had given me anything new and exciting, all the boys that were interested in me were quite pathetic and immature. And none of the really hot guys paid much attention to me. Some checked me out, I prided myself in my pretty looks and curvy figure. But none took it beyond that pathetic gawp that boys have. I was not that bothered, there was plenty of time for guys later on. In the meantime I was more than happy to enjoy myself with my friends.

Once, when my brothers and I were left allow with my grandmom who was asleep most of the day, we went into Delilah's room. We find a box with porn in it. Different kinds of magazines of people having sex. She even had rubber dicks and lotions. There were even pictures of Phyllisa and her in sexy nightwear. The scary part these bitches were fat as hell. The outfits looked like floss on them with no class. But the dirt was all the way at the bottom of the box, pictures of my cousins having sex with each other and men. I really didn't know if I should keep looking or threw up.

We took the magazines in our room. We started to go through the pictures. We were so excited that we cut out all the pictures we each liked and make our own little collages. It was so fun. It was the most fun we had in years. I picked all these crazy pictures of girl on girl action, white guys with big dicks, women and men in bondage.

After weeks and all the hard work, we put into our sex collages. The maid who my cousins had come over to clean that day. Just happened to find out collages. When we got home we got our ass beat, but it was all worth it.

Gil moved the edge of his chair and commenced to interrupt me, "I'm sorry that I have to interrupt Josephine but what age are you at this time?"

"I'll have to say I'll have to say I am 12 years old going on 13. Can I finish?"

"Please continue!"

"While let me tell you about my first girl on girl experience." The doctor was still sitting the edge of his chair with his notepad in his hand.

The "Girl"

There was a girl who lived a few doors down from me her name was Mia. She would come over almost every day to play or just to talk with me. She was quite shy at times, which I made her even cuter to the local boys.

I was painfully shy and embarrassed. Looking back, there were many guys who really liked me, but I was unable to flirt, as I didn't know how and I was terrified, literally. Mia actually was fun to play with and talk with.

The first time, I met my best friend was in 2007 when her family moved into the house next to us. I had been living in this house since

I was born, I had had many neighbors before her but none with kids. The first time I met her I new we would be friends.

Mia and I met a while back at Camp Fellowship in Millville but we weren't that close. We just happened go to the same church. We had some conversations here and there but they where never serious.

Then one day, when camp was ending, we hung out and had a couple camp events together. After, that camp ended, we didn't hang out for a while, but we would call each other to go grab something to eat or to go get our nails done, or something simple that lasted about an hour or two.

When, school started is when I learned the Mia had moved into my neighborhood but a few streets over. Mia and I had hand shakes, signals and secret languages, when we passed in the hallways at school. Mia's older sister Olivia would hang out with us too. Olivia was a bit older, but still one of us.

At one point, we just stopped hanging out until we met again at a middle school basketball game. Mia was invited by one of my classmates. Instead of going with him she decided to hang out with me the rest of the night. After, that game we started calling each other more often and were chilling every weekend. After, a little while we just started hanging out every day, and decided to be best friends.

In winter, we would have hot chocolate in the warmth. We do homework, sleepovers, and went to church together. We were inseparable. Nothing would be able to tear us apart. We two never felt the need of anyone else, rather no one felt comfortable enough when we were together. We always had our secret jokes and we preferred to keep them secret. Because some jokes when explained loses its essence.

My best friend was really important to me. We did everything together and every time I need her she's there for me just as I'm there when she needs me. Having Mia in my life was the best thing going. She never passed judgment on me nor did she make fun of me.

There were so many mean girls in my neighbor who got their rocks off making fun of others. But the same ignorant bitches were also leaving in the same neighborhood with more than just a brother and/or sister, mother, and father that lived with them. They always had jokes about how short my hair was, or how my cousins won't buy my brothers and me the latest new trends that was hitting *Bradless*. But thank God, Mia was different.

My best friend was everything to me, I never knew how close you can to a person so quick and end up caring for them so much. It felt good to know that I had someone there for me. Regardless of anything that happens. I knew she was going to be there and I could trust her, trust for me was not easy, everyone I meet had to earn my trust. And it was really important to know I had someone I could trust and depend on. Even though she and I fought once in a blue moon. She was still going to be my best friend regardless, because she was a really big part of my life and I loved her.

Girl on Girl Action

One afternoon, Mia came over my house. She wasn't her usual happy self. Apparently, her dad never showed up for their regular weekend visits. Mia was always wrapped into the latest gossip around the neighborhood. She always managed to keep me entertained by the drama. We just sat there in silence. After a few minutes of allowing him; to relax and fight about her father.

Out of nowhere, Mia kept looking at me. I really was getting weirded it, but I was curious to why.

"Why are you staring at me?"

"I was just thinking."

"About what?"

"Who else is here?"

"Just my grandmom and me….why?"

"Come with me and lock the door behind you.", as we ran to her house.

So, I did just that and follow Mia to my room. She stood before me, and I looked into her eyes for a very long minute. She swooned; biting her lip in a sexual manner as quickly turned around the closed the bedroom door. I really didn't know what she about to do. Then, she reached to the edges of my skirt and opened the back. There was nothing to interfere with the sight of my pussy peeking; from the bush that surrounded it.

She leaned forward with her hands on the insides of my thighs, and put the tip of her tongue at the top of my luscious slit. There wasn't really enough room to get any further so she dropped her hand behind my right knee. She lifted me up until she was forced me to balance for a moment on one leg as she set her foot beside me on the chair. I was inexperienced and horny as fuck.

Then the eating began in earnest. I knew could feel me trembling as I began to get close to climaxing when I just relaxed, and finally I was forced to put my hands on her head and steady myself to keep from falling as I came.

When I was done, she stood in front of me. I could feel her warmth pressed against me. The softness of her breasts pressed against my chest rose more than my spirits.

I had pulled her blouse open wide enough to bring one of her nipples to my lips and had sucked on it enough to make it hard. Then she undresses me. I have never stood naked in front of another woman before. She then ordered me onto the bed.

Mia tied me down to the bedposts. Mia began to plunge her finger in and out of my pussy. I was becoming wet. I tried to get my pussy to stop, but the more Mia's finger thrust into me, the wetter I became.

Mia pulled her finger out, coated with my pussy juice. She then put her moist fingertip in her mouth to taste my vaginal secretions.

"Your pussy sure is tasty, like a fresh Georgia Peach."

A shiver rippled up and down my spine, and my pussy seemed to steam. I began to whimper softly. There was that familiar tingle in my pussy, and I could feel my clit swelling, distending into throbbing hardness.

I choked back a squeal, not wanting to come, not wanting my best friend to know that I was going to have an orgasm from what she were doing to me. Nevertheless, I couldn't prevent it.

My hips were thrusting now, moving back and forth, grinding within the limits of the ropes. Mia plunged her finger in and out of my pussy faster and faster, feeling it suck and squeeze it. My clit was throbbing visibly, and I was crying with shame, yet with Fantasy Showbar, too. My pussy had betrayed me and there was nothing I could do about it. My face was flaming with shame, and my hips thrust back and forth, fucking on her finger. The orgasm increased, and I cried out as I began to come a second time.

After, I was released from my bondage, still in a bewildered state of mind I had stood before was my best friend for last six years without trying to conceal my very naked body. I felt as if she had degraded me, cum juice running down my thigh, my pussy was quivering and feeling as if those fingers were still jabbing into my vagina. We cleaned and made sure that we didn't leave an evidence of what had happened. I walked Mia out. Just as she was leaving she leaned over in whispered in my ear then pulled away and smiled.

As soon as I closed the door, I went straight to the bathroom and ran a tub of very hot water, hoping it would wash away my shame. I soaked in the bathtub; my mind was spinning with what had just happened to me at my best friend's house.

Mia last words to me played over in my head "Aaliyah, I'm gonna play this game with you again soon!" is what she whispered in my ear. It kept echoing through my head. I knew Mia would do these lewd acts with me again and I was totally powerless to stop it. I should report her to the proper authorities or my cousins/ grandmom, but they might send her to juvenile detention or worse, take her away from me.

I could never bear to be apart from my beloved best friend no matter what she did to me.

I felt very vulnerable inside. My vulnerability made me that much more sexy, beautiful and appealing to my best friend.

The New Attitude

As a child, I satisfy my feelings of lust through playing. I created fun situations and truly celebrate life. While I grew up, I was taught that I should not follow these wild desires. Having lust in our hearts and minds was a sin and we were always reminded that we were going to hell, if we do so.

I should always behave. I shouldn't do run

around naked or expose myself in anyway. I should pretending everything is great and dandy in our house. It was a fucking nightmare. The only time I felt normal and accept it was, when I was with Mia. I didn't feel comfortable with the kids of the neighborhood. It was always Mia and me against the world.

My birthday weekend

This time I was over Mia's house. No one was home. Part of me was hoping to do what we did before but I was nervous as hell. Mia invited into her room. I walked passed Mia and she closed and locked the door behind her.

Mia stood behind me for a moment before she stroked her wet hands along the sides of my body, becoming more adventurous her hands reached around and explored my breasts, caressing and touching me. One of her hands sensitively stroked my right breast, while she played the other hand, with the small gold ring in my naval.

Taking her hand from my breast for a

moment Mia moved my long hair to one side and began kissing and nibbling the nape of my neck. Standing up in middle of her room Mia's hands once more reached around me. She began gently squeezing my rapidly hardening nipples.

After a minute of having her hard nipples rubbed and caressed, I turned my body to face Mia and we kissed passionately, our tongues sliding in and out of each others opened mouths, while our hands explored each others breasts. Mine felt Mia's nipples standing hard and erect, like my own and my pussy tingled at the touch of Mia's breasts.

I slid my hand down Mia's body; my fingers passed Mia's naval before I touched Mia's neatly trimmed black pubic hair. Moving my hand still further, I ran my hand between her legs feeling the lips of her soft, smooth pussy. My index finger ran back and forth across Mia's lips, while the palm of her hand inadvertently stimulated her aroused clit.

Mia felt her getting very aroused by this slow and soft stroking and with a last kiss pulled herself away from mine. Standing a couple of feet from me, she lifted her right hand, smiled and beckoned me with her index finger. Then she walked backward and continually beckoned me as she made her way to the edge of the bed; I followed eagerly. Once Mia was close to the edge of the bed she let herself lie back on the edge of the bed, took hold of the bed post with one hand and opened her legs.

I walked between Mia's legs, bent forward and placed my hands on the soft cheeks of Mia's cute ass. Lifting her ever so slightly, I craned her head forward still further and started to lick between her legs.

With my free hand, Mia lightly massaged her breasts while I squeezed her brown nipples.

Using my thumbs, I parted her lips and with my saliva-covered tongue dived into her wet pussy. With fast movements of my tongue I licked her soft lips and darted in and out of her pussy, I only stopped licking occasionally kissing her engorged clit.

"Oh, baby!"', Mia moaned and softly yelped as I rammed my tongue in and out of her.

Within minutes of this rapid tongue stimulation, she neared an orgasm, her soft moans developing into dull screams as I expert my tongue lashed in an out of her. Removing my hands from her breasts Mia began to finger her clit and within seconds, waves of orgasm, with her clit as the epicenter, surged through her body. She shuddered uncontrollably as they hit like mini explosions across her entire body and with a loud moan Mia came.

"Oh. . . Oh my god. . . No... Oooohh!", she screamed out.

Mia threw back her mane of black hair and felt the muscles deep in her pussy and thighs tingle as the orgasm pulsed throughout her whole body. As the full intensity of the orgasm died a little she snatched a glance down her body at me and saw that she was delightfully licking the juices dribbling out of her wet opening.

"Oh God, baby. . . I love you!" Mia interjected, between breaths, trying to mentally slow her racing pulse.

I acted as if I didn't hear the "I love you" comment. I didn't feel the same and I wasn't going to tell her that now before she didn't take care me. I looked up from between Mia's legs, my face, chin dribbling with Mia's juices, and smiled. With the musky scent of Mia's pussy rolling through my nostrils, I looked deeply into Mia's eyes and smoothly said," Your turn!" I wiped my face on a nearby shirt.

Without making any remark. She pushed me and darted her tongue inside my very sensitive wet pussy. Mia starting slowly and softly tongued me, knowing that it would not take much to make me come repeatedly. As she gradually built up speed with her tongue, she resumed to finger of her the tip of my super sensitive clit. She took her two fingers and slowly inserted them inside my tight wet pussy as she continued to tongue me. With gradually increasing speed, she rhythmically thrust in and out of pussy using her tongue and fingers.

With so much stimulation between my legs, my arousal hit the roof once more. Pure passion raced through my veins once again, all my muscles went into spasm as I unleashed a huge scream and I tried to control my orgasm as I felt it run away like a rocket. I felt my body writhing under the pressure of the orgasm within.

Breathing erratically, I tried once again to bring my body under control. Still writhing and moaning between breaths that I could feel my body begin to come back under her control.

We stop and looked each and laughed. I was seamless. We hooked up whenever we could and we had the privacy by the end of the summer there were plans for her to move just in time for her to start her new school in a whole different town we have one last fling that August.

The last time

Mia came over who broke the news to me today that she was moving further down south Jersey with her parents. They found a really good Ivy League school to go to. I felt lost I didn't know what it was going to do without her around.

She was a great friend and a nice experiment to have fun with. I felt lost when she moved away. She moved away by the end of month of August. I kind of isolating myself a little bit despite that I was getting picked on and bully. I kept to myself a lot. I really did know what to do.

Chapter Six

Parting ways

Things were changing in our little dysfunctional home. My cousin Delilah moved out. She took her family and headed to Philly with her little family. Her fucked up boyfriend JB was finally release from jail after serving 15 years out of his 30 year sentence for weapons/ unlawful possession of two fired arms, drug paraphernalia, grand theft, assault, and kidnapping. Most of us will never see the inside of a jail, but JB that was really all he knew for 16 on. JB was an asshole, I really thought he was trying to bed hard. Deep down he had so many horror stories about jail and spending most of his time in solitary. You could tell he had a lot of dark secrets. Just by the look in his eyes.

Something about him didn't click. He was rocking a thick gold chain and his chest hair was poking out his bright blue satin shirt. He also was wearing winkle picker boots with Cuban heels, and hip-hugging elephant bell-bottoms. He looked like he was straight out of the 70's.

He wasn't even out that long before he was drinking and getting high. Thank God they weren't staying here. I don't have to deal with her and damn "little perfect family." Everyday my other cousin Phyllis just seem to be getting more and more distant anymore. She was always working or partying, she was barely home.

Church Life

I looked forward to every Sunday my grandma and cousin made us go to church so I thought it was wrong cuz they always got to stay home. I would leave for church 8:30am then we didn't return home until 3:30pm, it's like being in school since I thought it was torturement but that was a nice treat away from the family.

It was like being in school 6 days a week and only one day to enjoy being a kid. We did Sunday School that would last until about 9:30am. Then there was a little break between it before church started and then we would sit upstairs until the pastor got to a point in his program, were all of the children of church would up front of the church.

The pastor would come down from the pulpit and talk to us children and then I still don't go downstairs and sit in children church. This went on for years but just became like a punishment. The older I got, the more it just seem like hell. Another worst thing I started to notice that there was more gossip going on in the church. I heard less about God's word.

I start to resent going to church, so my best friend and I will always skipped out of church. We always loved hanging out at the nearby railroad tracks that led behind the church and all the way downtown. We would always return back right before church ended, so I could take the bus home and she could go home with her family. I only got to see her maybe once a month, because she lived in Browns Mills and I was farther away then from where I live but it was always nice to have someone to talk to.

Damien Lewis

Now, even some the church boys were trying to rape me and I was being molested by another secretly weirdo, who I had a crush on Damien Lewis from day one he had a crush on me too. I really confused about him always touching me. He wasn't all the good looking. I think the idea of nobody wanting to date him was more appealing.

I first met Damien at a pot luck dinner during my practice at church for the Christmas play. He was cracking jokes and making everyone laugh. He seemed like such a fun guy. He was also a Christian, the perfect package.

Damien had brown, curly hair tight in a ponytail reveals a furrowed, lively face. Woeful blue eyes, set lightly within their sockets, watch gratefully over the country they've felt at home at for so long. Dark stubble delightfully compliments his mouth and leaves a delightful memory of his fortunate looks. He stands elegantly among others, despite his tough frame. There's something bewildering about him, perhaps it's a feeling of guilt or perhaps it's simply his fortunate past.

Damien knew which path, he would be taking in his future career. He had planned on becoming a reverend in the future. He wanted to serve God, but deep down Damien was just like any other boy going through puberty. We would say that but in private we were two kids learning.

Damien was older than me by four years. He had an older brother named Raymond who was likable and affable man. He was widely respected in the community, charming and easy to get along with. He was a good Baptist and sharp businessman who, when not working with his father.

There were rumors were starting to spread around town, about Ray's sexual preferences, but no one dare to ask any questions. But something about Raymond always creepied me out, just the way he looked at me. He was hanging out with his brother. He also spent much of his free time hosting elaborate street parties for with his friends and neighbors.

Within a month, we were secretly talking. I was flattered that Damien wanted to pursue me and excited about the way he showered me with affection. He would send me flowers. He'd also buy me cards and write scripture mixed with professions of his love for me. I wanted to believe he was really sincere.

Just then, I stop talking to the doctor all I do was chuckled.

"What's the chuckling for?"

"Don't worry doctor, I will tell you everything in dues time. "I said it in a seduce way.

Gil just smiled.

Being taking advantage of

One day at church, I was coming out the ladies bathroom. There stood Damien in the little hallway. Before I could say a word or walk passed him. He forced me into the wall and kiss me hard. I didn't know what to do. I really didn't know how to handle it.

This was the first time, I ever kissed a boy. I also didn't want people knowing that I'm was messing with the church boy. He wasn't what you would call the most attractive guy in the entire church but it was kind of appealing here in there. I always had a thing for the oddballs. I was able to break free from his grip and head back upstairs.

I guess he was piss what I did. The following Saturday at the church's annual picnic. What happened next I wasn't expect to happen. Damien walked up to me and knocked me on to the ground. He tried to rape me right there in front of my entire family. The sad part was no one was watching to see it happen. I couldn't breathe. I couldn't fight as hard as I wanted to, he was so fucking heavy.

I picked up a handful of rocks and started throwing them at the table where my grandma was standing. My grandma turned around in a flash when rocks hit her. She saw him on top of me. She came running over and start to crack him over his back with her cane.

She kept me close to her side for the rest of

the day. I was so embarrassed and humiliated by what he did. Of course other church members were whispering under their damn breathe like as if I wasn't sitting there. I was young and he was a horny young man. He fucking embarrassed my family and me. I just wanted him to die.

Nightmare

He finally apologized to my grandmom and me. He asked my grandmom and cousin to take me out to dinner as long as his older brother was watching over us. My cousin thought it would good idea. My grandmom didn't agree. I agree with my grandmom. I wasn't feeling Damien. But my cousin pushed and win. So, the following week. It was a date. I was scared to death to see what he was up to.

Damien and his brother picked me up to go to the local diner. Ray dropped us off, leaving with Damien. Hopefully Damien won't do anything stupid. Over dinner, he told me that he loved everything about me, the way I dressed, my laugh, my relationship with God, the way I interacted with my girlfriends. We had a great evening so we continue to talk afterwards.

But it wasn't long before, he started to pick on the small things. One day, he decided he didn't like my best friend. So, I distanced myself from her. One night he didn't like the outfit I was wearing, so I changed. Another night he claimed I was wearing too much make-up. I went to the bathroom and washed it off. I couldn't win for shit with him. This motherfucker did a 360 on me and didn't know what I was doing wrong.

We'd go out to eat and Damien would smile at other girls. When, I would confronted him about it, he blew me off. Not only that, he would tell me what he liked about them, and how I lacked in comparison, such fucking asshole.

We were in a restaurant waiting to be seated. A woman was sitting at a table nearby with her legs crossed. Damien commented on how long her legs were, then he looked at mine and didn't say a word. But the point was clear. My legs didn't measure up. How could he say my legs weren't good enough? How could I change them?

At that point, I realized I couldn't take it anymore. I had tried to change everything about myself to please him, and now with something I couldn't change, insecurity overwhelmed me.

After, five long months, I decided to end our relationship. Damien was angry over my decision. He felt God had told him, we were to be married. What a fucking joke! I wanted to go to my girlfriends for support, but I had given them up months ago to please Damien. I suddenly felt very alone.

A few weeks later, Damien called and invited me out for dinner as friends, he said. Our time in the restaurant was awful. He was loud and obnoxious to the waiters and to me. I called everything to see if anyone could pick me up. The last person on my list I really didn't want to call was Damien's brother Raymond.

Ray showed up 15 minutes after I called

home. He drove me back to home after dinner, I didn't object. I was more than ready for the evening to end. I was happy to get away from Damien. Unfortunately, Ray didn't intend to drive me home. He took me to a deserted parking lot and raped me.

"Ray, why are we here?"

"I am going to do what my brother wasn't able to do."

"What the fuck are you talking about?"

I slowly back into the door. I try to grab on the handle. It was missing. I went to rolled down the window. No luck! I try to fly across him to get out his door. He slammed me in my seat. He forced himself on me. He was too strong for me. The harder, I fought back the more he gaining control over me. I was losing and I was devastated.

I looked away from him The car windshield covered with fog, the struggle, and the moment I felt too overpowered to resist any longer. I screamed at him to stop. He wasn't listening. When, he was reaching for his pants, I keep pulling his hand away.

At some point, he pulled his hand back up from his pants he pulled out his belt, and wrapped it around my neck. He pulled it tighter the more I fought. He laughed in my face as he did so. He tried kissing and keep moving my face away from him. He punched me in my face and commence to beat me. I was now weak to fight back. There wasn't anything I could do about it. I had so many abrasions on my body. I hurt everywhere.

Before, I knew it he jerked my clothes off from the waist down. He had taken off my underwear, his fingers had been inside of me. I don't even know this person who forcing a way on me. I hate my cousin made see this guy in the first place. She probably knew this was going too happened. In that instant I realized there was nothing I could do to stop what was happening. He was simply too strong.

He put my legs over his shoulder and throw his entire weight down on me, making it impossible for me to move. The look in his face was of serial killer *Ted Bundy,* when he was smiling in court. His breathing was of *John*

Wayne Gacy with his fat face. His breath was hot and nasty ass fuck. His eyes were dark.

He was grunting and making disgusting faces at me. There was an evil look, I never seen before. As, he thrust harder into me, with each stuck he blew mud out of ass, which flew all over the car window. I wanted to throw up so bad. My stomach was saying, help me, help me.

It felt like it was hours, but it only lasted a few minutes. When it was over, I jumped up and got dressed. Ray fell back in the driver's seat. Ray took off his wife beater and wiped the shit off his window. I felt so dirty. I wanted to washed the scent of this motherfucker off of me. Ray wasn't even taking back from what he did. He could see it on his smug face that he enjoyed what he did. He sat there trying catching his breath.

Ray fixed his clothes. He had the fucking nerve to look at me laughing, "Look what what you made me do! I strongly suggest you keep this between us or else!"

I really didn't know what to do at this point. He would tell Damien to give me a call, with this devilish smile on his face. If I jumped out now I would either die out here or get lost I had no idea where I was. I kept my mouth shout and got dress.

It was complete silence as he took me back home. He simply pulled away from the curve, after slapped his car door, he smile and drove off like he was a fucking king of the world. I was in shock.

All I remember about those following hours as I was standing in the shower with all my clothes on, sobbing uncontrollably, as I hoped that no one heard. I desperately wanting the water to wash away the evening's events and the filthy scent of him off me. I stood there examining my body beneath the stream of water and decided, I don't want my body anymore. I was terrified of it. I felt contaminated.

I never told my grandma or my cousins, I kept it to myself. I was afraid that if I reported it I would embarrassed my family. My cousin would have went fucking crazy over the news. I could not digest or accept any of this information. I could not imagine my family having to read about this online or the newspaper.

Things were getting bad. I couldn't sleep anymore. I was constantly tossing and turning. When, I did fall asleep, I would wake up 4 hours later with it fresh in my mind. I was having nightmares and flashbacks. I started showing signs of depression. I was having difficulty concentrating no matter what I was doing.

The rape has got me on the edge, never trusting every corner I walk around. I had to sit with my back to the wall, so I can see everyone that come. Every where, I went I watched the person who walked in and walked out of the stores, restaurants, and my classrooms. I would try to remember the color of their skin, even their eye color, and make their clothes.

I didn't want to be touched by strangers. Scared to be near anyone that I wasn't close. If weren't in my circle, I didn't want anyone near me. feared that I may lose control. My anger was growing me; it was taking over me some days.

I felt like a whole different personality was running through my system. I didn't know how much longer I could take this and control the person I was becoming, but the person in me wants to seek revenge. I can't hear much but deep inside I could hear a faint voice ramping, screaming, and yelling. I don't know what to do.

I started to develop this annoying thing of rubbing my left ear loop. Things just seemed to disappeared at times. The storm within me would calm down but that didn't last for long before everything would start all over again.

I was becoming that person who was afraid to even open my bedroom door to go to the bathroom. I was sitting in my bedroom constantly rocking back and forth in my slider chair. There was a combination of numbers that was rolling in my head. I could hear the voices, but could never really making out what they were saying. They were whispering over and over. I would just jump back in my bed in fetus position crying.

The voices.....these voices.....these fucking voices are getting louder. They are becoming more clear each day. I find myself rubbing war more. I have headaches to four times a day. They won't stop. Thoughts of suicide, horniness, killing, and wanting to crawl up in ball and cry.

I really wanted to take a bullet to my head to stop the voices. They were whispering over and over. I would just jump back in my bed in fetal position crying. Rubbing my ear and within a few minutes later, I am much calmer and in control. I finally fall right to sleep.

I couldn't sleep alone at night without having a light on or the television on, like I was a fucking five year old child, because I had almost nightmares almost every fucking night of being touched where I cannot wake up. I did this thing where I waited until the sun came up and I felt safe enough to sleep. For three months, I went to bed at six o'clock in the morning, then I had to be in school by 8am. It was hard.

I find myself at night lying in my bed all alone in the darkness, looking up to the ceiling window, as the tears falling out of my face, trying to be quiet so my grandma and brothers wouldn't hear me cry. I hate it! I just want to die. I want teaching the bully of your schoolmates and being raped I didn't feel clean. I felt so dirty scrubbing you taking 3 showers a day wasn't helping

I felt guilt, shame, self-blame, embarrassment, fear, distrusting anyone and everybody, and sadness. I was very vulnerable and very isolation from the world. I tried to push it out of my mind, but it was so heavy I didn't talk, I didn't eat, I didn't sleep, I didn't interact with anyone. I would be the alone at times it was the best time for me to scream.

I never know which day is going to be a good day or bad day depending on how I feel when I wake up. Some days, it's great not a single negative thing to pop up in my head, nothing to stop me from doing what I have to get done. But sometimes by the end of the night, I lay in my bed tossing and turning as flashes of that night continue to haunt me, leaving me in tears. I found myself in the same position I fell asleep in with a ball of wet tissues in my hand.

Chapter Seven

Being bully/ suicide attempt

I started this self-sabotaging habit where, even though I had endless potential and teachers told me, "You're such a bright young lady, and you have all these opportunities." I would always rolled my eyes at the teachers as if they were talking out of their necks. The fucking girls from my damn school who tried to start shit from time to time, we continue to fight until someone comes to break up the fights each time. Whether it was intentionally or subconscious. I would do all my studying and do fine on tests academically, but when it came to actually doing homework or projects, I just would slack and turn them in late or when I felt like it.

I was digging myself into this huge hole, and it just exacerbates this self-loathing and this depression. It's like, here I am at the bottom of this hole. I felt trap I have no idea where to go, where to begin, no one to run to, and no one to talk too.

Right now, I only seen as a solution to end this bullshit. I can't get out, and I can't do anything about it. I finally got the nerve to go the police department. I gave them my statement from start to finish. They took pictures of me, names of my closest friend, and I even turned in my clothes from that night. I never washed them I threw them in a trash bag and threw them in the back of my clothes.

I returned home and felt even more dirty. I wanted to die. I was suppose to see a counselor and psychologist to get this. It was getting to the point I wanted to end this. Screaming at the top of my lungs, hoping no one would hear me.

My anxiety levels were starting to go through the roof, so I ended up calling my psychologist and tell him what was going on. I don't have the patience to go to the hospital. Fucking embarrassing, everyone looking at me as if I was fucking crazy. I couldn't find any cure for my sickness or the loneliness I was facing. I felt trapped.

Some days, it's so bad I turn off the phone. I disconnect myself from the world. I locked myself in my room. I'm tried to watch movies that will keep me occupied. Only to I find myself staring down my the staircase of my room. I don't know, if it's just my vision or whatever is going on, As listen to my heart beat, I can see the top of my stairs and my posters on my wall; the whole room was sway, but every time I inhale and exhale my surrounds sway with each heart beat. I close my eyes and hope that I fall asleep, but the voices are just overpowering my thoughts, my sleep, my everyday life, and everything is getting to me, I don't want to do.

He decided to put me on Lorazepam to help with my anxiety attacks. The rape was eating my soul away. I can't take it anymore. I was finding myself losing control never want to be outside always crying stuck in a room. Now, stuck on my anxiety pills. They want me to be a fucking zombie. Nothing else feels like anymore home, only in my head. I still have breakthrough attacks. I swear they need to up the doses in my pills. Some days they feel like they don't work for shit. I want to be free. I want to quit, let the voices take over. I am fighting a fight I can't win. My nerves are rattle just by the sound of a clock, caused me to shake. A piercing pain shots through the left side of my head causing my left eye to roll back enough to see the white in them.

Numbness can be the best feeling in the world going through life not knowing, not understanding and not caring for a damn thing in the world. I always pop another cycle of dramatic pills into your system. No more pain so I would not feel the emotions that controlled the best and the bad days.

I never understanding, if I was coming or going and numbness allows me to build a wall when shit starts to explode. I pop another pill maybe one and a half two times a day to keep the demons at bay. I think I am able to control what I can. Before time runs out and it's time to pop another one to one and a half pill that day but catching when I'm off of it. It could be unladen you with so many things or she can turn your life into a shit storm.

Laying in my bed or when I'm at work I find myself cussing and screaming in my head wishing I can scream louder but I gotta keep it quiet. The random thoughts never stop. I didn't want my coworkers to learn anything about me. The voices were getting stronger and louder. I feel myself slipping away. I don't know what to do. Just hearing my own voice makes me sound like I'm crazy. I know I'm batshit crazy, but maybe it is for the best numbing the pain with all that I have. I could wash them out with pills each day. I was secretly trying to hide the truth trying to cover the pain that was called but the fuel in my heart and my guts. Each day, the voices were getting clearer. What was I to do? Was I going to allow those voices to take over or fight to keep them at bay?

I couldn't stand being me. I can't imagine this fucking person anymore. I just fucking wanted to end this so call life I have. So fucking tired of being bullying and people fucking with me. These so called family members and friends who molested and raped me. Be bullying by those same assholes.

My cousins and all the boys in neighborhood, I have come across thinking I'm just a piece of meat. Even some of my family members treated me like I was odd ball. I can't keep friends but at the same time I don't want any. My parents are not around. I hate my family I was brought into. Why the fuck I even a live?

I was fighting with other classmates almost every other month, about not having parents or the way I looked. Fucking bitches would pull at the little bit hair I did have. I even poked out one of my bully's eye. I never felt sure pleasure of seeing her scream and kicking around with one in. I just stood over her smiling. Thank God I wasn't at school when it happened.

"Why's that Aaliyah?"

"I'm not Aaliyah! You still haven't figured out who is talking?"

"Tasha?"

"Yes, now back to what I was saying!"

"When do you really pop into Aaliyah's life?"

"During this time in her life, it's here and

there. I usually pop out when Aaliyah is in middle of a fight or upset. Aaliyah fights me a lot but she still isn't aware of all the personalities."

"Ohhh, I see, now!"

I'm so alone. This world is so fucking cruel. I just want to die. I feel so insecure no matter what I do. Every person I thought was my friend, just as fake as they want to be. She was so quick to lie and steal from me. She was fucking bougie, acting like her shit didn't stink.

One day, I couldn't take it. I made a lynch making sure it was short so I wouldn't touch the ground when I dropped. I attached to the beam that was in an over head crawl space in my room. I made sure it was tight. I crawled into the crawl space. I put it around my neck and before I dropped and I asked God to please forgive me.

I fall out of the crawl space. I was hanging there for a minute before the rope snapped. I grasped for air. There was a knock at my door. I pulled the lynch off my neck just in time before the door opened. I played it off like nothing happened and ran downstairs to help him.

A few weeks later, I tried to kill myself by putting myself under the water when I went to take my daily bath. I wasn't able to stay to long under before my cousin walked to use the bathroom. She just looked at me when she came in and sat her fat ass on the toilet. I quickly let out the water, jumped out of the tub and went to my room. I guess I should just quit.

I used to be pride of myself on my independence, now I am afraid to go on walks in the evening, to attend social events. Damien kind of disappear after everything. I try to fight myself from doing harm to myself. I joined the school orchestra and started playing the violin. I went through middle school numb must of thing. My brothers were getting in more and more trouble. With my grandmom and Delilah no longer at the house, it made so much easier to get away shit.

Moving Forward

I was tuning my violin for my youth group worship when my friend Olivia ran up excitedly. "Hey, Aaliyah," she said. I looked up, I was ready to pop off to yell at my friend but I stop and thought, because I wasn't Aaliyah, I was Tasha. I took over because Aaliyah just couldn't handle things. I just went along with it.

Olivia yelled, "I got my roll of pictures from our church's annual picnic developed. I thought you'd like to have this one, because there was one of me the violin." as she continued to walked towards me, waving a picture in the air.

I glanced at the photo. "Wow, that's great," I said, smiling. "Thanks!"

As, she went to find a seat, I slipped the photo into my violin case. Later that night, when I was alone in my room, I took the picture out and stared at it. I hated it. I look so hideous, I thought. I was so small, my violin looks like a little toy. I want to be a musician? Who's heard of a toothpick rock star?

I'd been underweight for as long as I could remember. Now, I was one of the smallest girls in my junior class in high school. I hated being the best friend and never the girlfriend. I hated being the funny girl, people laughed at and not the cool girl, they envied. I want to be more than the happy go lucky slim girl, I thought. I am tired of being the best friend. I am done with this.

I decided that if I wanted be better I going to work out more, I just ate less. So early that winter of my junior year, I started cutting back. Within weeks, I was eating more and more. Some days at lunch, I'd eat junk food. Soon, I'd gained ten pounds. I was so happy. Wow, this is working. I thought. Now, if I was able to get my hands more food without Phyllisa realizing food was missing. I will be that much closer to where I want to be, in size.

Chapter Eight

Senior Year

By the first day of my senior year, I was a new woman. I came back as a new person. I start over with who I was. Still showing that innocent look but at the same time becoming the diabolical bitch people wish they fucked with.

I was looking forward to this year moving through the senior year with my head straight. Trying to stay focus on my new goals. I know what I want. I want to get the hell up out of the house as soon as possible. I haven't even decided what colleges, I want to go to. I'll be eighteen soon and I don't have to be under the reign of my cousin's bullshit anymore. Aaliyah couldn't be the person we needed anymore.

Gil quickly moved to the edge of his chair and shifted his body towards me as he asked as if he was lost, "I'm sorry I have to stop you there! What gives you the right to take over?"

This fucking doctor trying my fucking patience. I popped my head and rolled my eyes at him as I replied back, "Have not been listen DOCTOR??"

"Yes, I have!"

"Then what's the fucking problem?"

"I was curious to what happened to Aaliyah?"

"Well, then you need to shut the fuck up! You would learn a thing or two."

Gil sat back in his chair and just listened. As, I started back up.

We are tired deal with the bullshit that has been inflicted on Aaliyah and us. Every fucking day, it was tearing us up. Aaliyah is trapped in her own little box. Nothing more than cage with images playing over and over, as she cry over the bullshit. We are not taking anymore shit from anyone. Now it's our time to dream and fucking live!

As, I walk through the hallway on the first day of school and I noticed somebody. I still wasn't sure if my mind was treats on me. I can't believe it! Someone from my past, now is at my school. Between classes, I keep seeing this person but I needed to get closer to make sure.

To be honestly, I am hoping that this person isn't who I thought it was. I commenced to ask around, I learned that he was our new football coach. He transferred here from Washington High School. I didn't know his classes. I let it go for now. I had to play it careful. I don't want draw any attention to myself.

I wasn't going to let this guy get away from me, without making sure that this was or wasn't the same asshole. But, I'm pretty sure it was. Just when, I wanted to call it quits for today. There he was walking past me in same the hallway. I glanced away at my books before I got a chance to look back up. I collided into someone.

My books flied on out my arms. I almost

lose balance. I was able to catch myself. I bend over to get my books. I pushed my glasses back onto my face. A hand reached to had me a book. I look up and there he was Raymond. That was the son-of-a-bitch who fucking raped me.

Raymond said, "Sorry about that!"

I caught myself from flipping out because right then and there I realize that he didn't recognize me. I played it off and apologized for my part. I wanted to fucking pull his heart out of his chest. I couldn't do it right now. I could feel my blood boiling. He put out his to shock hands. I really didn't want to, but I did.

"What is your name?

I looked him in his eyes, put a fake smile on my face, tilted my head to left a little bit, and said Aaliyah.... Aaliyah Churchill." I really wanted to give the wrong name. But I already knew that he would find out.

"That's a pretty name!

"Thank you and your name is?"

"Coach Raymond Lewis"

"That's cool. Who are you coaching?"

"I'm the new football coach."

"Oh, okay! While I have to head to class. I am late."

"What class are you heading to?

"Calculus"

Just then he pulled out a pad and started to write something. "Here is a pass. This should help you."

I took the pass and thanked him. Oh my goodness, this motherfucker has no idea who I am! I wanted snap his fucking neck, but this may work out to my advancement.

"Well, I hope to see again!"

"That would be nice!"

I grabbed the rest of my stuff and headed to class. I continue with the rest of my day. I don't remember what half of my teachers were talking about in class.

Over the next few weeks, I was able to find out his classes, and his habits. Now, he was more of a fucking douche bag than I remember. Raymond and I talked outside school. We never talked on the phone or over the computer. Since, he just happen to be practicing during my gym class, on the days he wanted me come over to his condo that was across town away from prying eyes. I was actually glad, because I didn't want anyone to know anything about me.

He would wear a red polo shirt with the Tanzanian Devil on his left pocket. The fucker even gave me a key to get in and the code to the alarm. He didn't want people getting the wrong idea about us.

Which, I already knew was bullshit. He claims it was, because he was going through a nasty divorce and custody battle over his teenage daughter. This actually work in my favorite. When we did meet up Josephine had to step in. Josephine always find a excellent excuse why they couldn't have sex yet. He actually believed her. She did make out with him. Sometimes, even allowing him to give him face or play with her pussy and ass.

Finally a few months later, I finally gave into his bullshit. We made plans to go up north to the cabins, during our summer break. That was perfect. I made plans to go to Pennsylvania to visit my godmother and family. I told him I would make all the arrangements. He was worried about me using a credit card. He gave me $2,000 to set everything up. The motherfucker just sign his death wish.

I kept my tabs on him learning as much could. I was thinking of ways to get even. He made me sick to talk to him, but Josephine made it easy by stepping in and helping me out. To make things even more interesting I became good friends with his one and only daughter. The wheels were rolling in my head, but I had to be careful.

Nadia was a freshman at the same high school. She had black, shaggy hair almost fully covers a fine, anguished face. Lidded hazel brown eyes, set well within their sockets, watch impatiently over the her surroundings. She was always on guard.

She later confide to tell me she was being molested by her father and how much she hated him. I promised to keep quiet, but I was even more pissed off. I kept my promise. I kept her secret. The more I learned about her father, the more I wanted to seek revenge for the both of us. I couldn't share my secret, especially with Nadia. It would destroy my plans.

The more I learned about her father and

what he was doing to her. It had piss me off even more, making this revenge much deeper than I expected to be. This man was a fucking monster and now I made it my mission to get even, but I don't know how to go about everything. I commenced to do a research on ways to get even. The great thing was I taking criminal justice classes. No one even suspect anything. You're probably thinking I should have called the cops and did the right thing but it seems like doing the right thing anymore in this world, it's not good enough.

He would get a slap on the wrist, maybe probation little bit of time and he'll go back doing the same fucking damn thing to another woman another child in another state covering his tracks and change and everything that he does is seen it a thousand times. Who are they going to believe a bunch of girls or the towns hero, the coach everybody loves.

Taste for Killing

The more I thought about getting even with

Raymond, the more I yearn to kill. I started to get this urge to kill something or someone, but I've never killed anyone. Nor have I ever touched a knife to someone's throat. Nor have I seen anyone die in front of me. For the first time, I wanted to flip and cause pain on someone else.

I try controlling my urges. I really don't know how to stop. I found myself dreaming of killing people and waking up finding that I was touching myself aroused and turned on about the thought of someone dying. There were days, we let Aaliyah step in, despite the fact that she has no idea what is going on.

"Why do you let Aaliyah step in?"

"Are you paying attention?"

"Yes, I'm paying attention I just want to make sure I have everything understandable!"

"All right look here I let her step in because it's easier to deal with the stupid shit and the harassment and all the drama that comes with it because I know me the minute somebody touches me the minute somebody pushes my button I'm ready to snap and I'm trying to control all these urges I'm starting to get and Josephine is sexually she wants to be she handles all the sexual shit. I really don't know why you keep asking as if you're dumb but it's alright stupid is as stupid does!"

"I'm sorry I just want to make sure I get all my facts straight. I know you're asking a lot of questions why I just want to make sure I'm on the same page as you are."

One day during lunch, I was hanging out with Nadia. She had something weird that she wanted to show me. As soon as, I heard that I made sure Aaliyah was put back in here corner. I needed to be careful. She wanted me to meet her by the creek which was a couple blocks from my house.

So, later on that evening after dinner, as planned I walk down to the creek and I met with Nadia. I heard cats meowing, but I don't see where they were. It was curious to see what she was up to but if the bitch tried me, I was going fuck her up.

"I see you made it!"

"Yeah, well you said, You had something to show me I wanted to see what you had in store. What is up with those damn cats?"

"You will see that they keep running the neighborhood. We are infested with so many unwanted animals. I got two of them."

"Oh that's cute of you."

"No, I fucking hate cats do you like cats now my mom loves cats. We have so many cats in our neighborhood. I'm just so sick of them. I don't even think the neighborhood would notice if a few cats come up missing. I brought you down here for a disappearing act.

"Now, you are magician?' I was being to think this bitch is more fucking crazy than I was.

"I have a magic trick to show."

"Whatever! Humor me!"

She pulls one that cats out by its neck. She commenced to wrap duct tape around its mouth just enough so it could still breath. Then she laid the cat down on its back and caressing its stomach. I had no idea where the hell this was going. Nadia pulled out a pocket knife commenced to stab the knife into the cat's throat. The cat went completely limp. I didn't even know what to say, but at the same time it looked so cool.

Nadia looked at me with so much excitement

in her eyes. With a smile on her face she said," Let's see what the cat looks like on the inside."

She began to cut open the each cat. She made an effort to reveal the cat's organs everywhere. She then put her hand in last cat's blood. As she stares back me, she rubs the blood on her face. I was afraid to say anything to her about how it was getting dark. God only knows what she's going to do the next. I was curious to see was going to happen next.

I was getting excited. This was more exciting and arousing. I try to hide my emotions. I can feel my nipples getting hard, This shit was getting me moist. I want thousand horror movies. I got excited watching this type of shit but to see it up close and in person.......wow.

With blood dripping down her face, she walked over to me and started to under me. She then smeared blood ll over my nake body. Feeling the warm blood on my was so fucking arousing. It took a lot out me to hide it.

There we were seating butt ass nake in the woods with the full moon shining down on us. I really didn't know what to do. Just then she told me to lay back and close my eyes. I didn't dare to ask, so I laid back, took a deep breath and close my eyes. I had no idea what she was up to. I felt this cool breeze sleep swept across my body. It felt so nice. take a deep breath and relax. Just then I felt a warm liquids being poured on me. I knew it was more cat blood. I wanted to rub it into my skin, but I just laid there. It felt soooo amazing!

"How does that feel?", She asked.

"It feels OK, I guess?" I replied. I really didn't want to tell her the truth.

As, the blood hit my nipple, I could feel it getting harder than ever before. I was getting aroused, the more blood she poured across my body. She let it drip down onto my stomach and down my legs. I couldn't take it anymore. I rubbed it in on my stomach.

Out of nowhere, she said," You like that, don't you?"

"All I could say was, "Yes."

I was curious and was wondering did I ever show sign, I wanted to kill someone. I really wanted to do it. I just never told her. I sat up and asked why me?"

"Well you seem like a cool person. I always notice, you especially when you wearing that nice mini red skirts. Every time you had on high heels, I wanted to spread those long legs open. I was disappointed to find out that you only like guys. I was surprise that we became friends. I also thought you were a witch like me.

"Oh wow! Why didn't use a black cat?"

"Black cats are sacred."

"Oh okay!" I didn't know what else to say. Then continue to talk about being a witch. I had no fucking idea why she would think that, but I knew that she was awakened darker inside of me. I kept talking about her being a witch, all honestly I really didn't give a fuck about her being a witch. I was more worry about keeping my cool and not revealing my intimate thoughts that flashing through my head.

I can feel my heart racing. I did my best to not show her but the warmth of the blood was turning me on. She shut up real quick when I spread your legs open. Josephine jumped because if this keeps talking and as much I was loving the warmth of the blood. She would have been next.

I'm not trying to fuck up my plans for this

bitch. I guess she was enjoy seeing me playing with myself. She slowly dripped some blood down my girl. She took her hand and started to play my clit as rub the blood into my juices and licked it cleaned off her fingers.

She dropped down onto her stomach. She buried her head between my legs. I didn't dare to stop her. I laid back clean all the blood off my girl. I came harder the more she buried her face further into my pussy. She kept licking and caressing my clit. Sticking her tongue in and out of my girl. I couldn't help it. I came right on her face and she licked every drop of blood off my girl and my cum.

I didn't know what to say to that I just sat there and shocked and embarrassed that I just allow my friend to go down on me and put cat blood on me. She sat down by side me. She started talking.

"I always want to do that to someone."

"What, lick blood or my pussy?"

"Both! You and your pussy taste so sweet!"

"Thank you, I guess!?!?" I was weird-ed out. I can say I have heard worse from others.

I really didn't have anything else to say to her. We jumped into the nearby lake to wash the blood off. I was more turn on about filling the cat's blood all over my body and then her licking it off of me. I didn't want her to know my inner secrets. I just told her that it felt good with her face down there.

I acted like that was my first time getting face. Which I knew was a lie, but I wasn't tell her that. She expressed that she wanted to eat me again. Hey, I'm not gay and she wasn't asking me to return the favorite. I didn't see anything wrong about me getting some face from time to time.

Once we were done, we got dress. For right now, I just did it when it was convenient for us to hung out. I gather as much dirty as I could about he father. I did my to not keep all my secrets to myself and what I was up to. Some times I want to stab a pencil in her neck this bitch talks to much. We let Aaliyah deal with her.

I see why she doesn't ave any friends. If wasn't for the juice information I was getting from her about her father. She would have been one of my victims. I have to suffer in silence.

At least she does a great job of giving face. Some day in order to get her to shut the fuck up. I either push her face in my pussy or ram my fingers into her.

I will say, after that night the thirst was driving me crazy. I NEED to calm the need. I became very good of hiding it. I had to find different hobbies to stay busy. I join some clubs at school, they only help for that moment but I start to wonder off. I didn't dare to share my thoughts and feeling with anyone. Allowing Aaliyah to step in. Aaliyah was the good girl and quiet.

She was and is so fucked up in the head. She never opened up to anyone, making our lives easy. Josephine and I really want to have fun and cause some chaos. Our time will come to kill something or someone. I decided to practice when I was alone and had time to do so.

The thirst is driving me crazy. I thrive to kill something or someone. It was beginning a second nature when was I had to do it just to kill the urge to kill the itch. If it wasn't that it was sex, but seeing her kill that cat tournament one in so many ways and I woken up something in me darling.

I could never ever guess between Josephine and myself, we're starting to take over. We were her dominating people anytime. Josephine, you need to step in for anything sexual. She got to enjoy as I sat there and watch we were a team. Josephine was my best friend and I loved her. Aaliyah...... what a fucking wimp. We had to take over. We couldn't let her keep doing this. I knew exactly who was going to be my first victim.

Some days after school, I find myself back in the words, taking my interest and hatred out on defensiveness animals. I first practiced my butchery by cutting up dogs and cats and impaling their heads on sticks. I once put a cat in a pillowcase and throw medium size rocks at it. I wanted to see how much it could take. After twenty minutes I would let it out, watching it slowly crawl out. I then kicked it into the lake only to watch the struggle drain. Different ideas on how to kill people was flashing through my head more often. I went on to burn another cat alive, stone dogs and cut off rabbits' heads. At night I would tie rabbits to railway lines to watch them be run over. I took the time, to catch animals in a noose, poisoned or hanged.

Chapter Nine

My First Killing

The day finally came, I was so excited but I wanted to take my time. I didn't show any signs of being suspicious about anything. I kept my cool so the day I left school early and headed up to the cabin. I set it up I told him to meet me there at 6pm for a special dinner and a movie. I even had enough to dig up 10 foot hole, that was 3 feet away from cabin in the backyard.

I got our father's favorite machete cleaned up just for this occasion. It is a rare token that he left behind that was hidden from the family from all these years. Somehow I was able to get into that house and keep it away from my cousins. Today was a perfect time to pull it out I had sharpened it and clean it to the finals. I can see my reflection in it. Even hide a few mini cameras to get the perfect angles of this beautiful events.

I put on my best fuck me outfit on and waited for his arrival as I cooked dinner. It was almost time for Josephine to step in. Well, I prepped the proper delicious meal for him. Just think, this will be his last meal and he doesn't know it. At 5:45pm, there was a knock on the door. I had to fix myself before opening the door.

Raymond actually arrived promptly with some garden weed flowers. They looked like he picked them from his grandma's backyard, they were tacky as fuck. I don't know who he was fooling. If he only knew who I was and what is stored in for him. I went to go fix us a drink and he walked to the dining room. He was impressed with all the fixings and everything that was on the table. Just like that I watched him take my plate and his plate and did a quick switch, but it's okay. Because I had giving myself his plate that laced with some drugs. I got him right were I want him. He did me a favorite.

I knew that he loved red meat and since he was a workout junkie. I made sure that he had all the right fixings for athletic man like him There was enough food for his weight and then some. I wanted to make sure I had the right mixture of everything to get his taste buds going, I can get all the drugs that I needed into his system enough to seduce him.

Time to Eat

We all sat down for dinner. We laughed and talked while we ate. Raymond was started to shows of the pills kicking in. It was almost time for Josephine to kick in. I made a pass at just to see how twisted fucked-up he was and he took the bait. He took it and being the person I am, I beginning to put the rest of plan in motion. Josephine kicked in. She got up from the table and commenced to walk over to Raymond.

She pulled out his chair from underneath table. He tried to pull her in for a kiss. She refused to kiss him knowing the drugs where in his bloodstream and probably a residue on his lips. she didn't want to get any in hers. She was keeping us all focus on what our plans were.

Josephine was enjoy him. Josephine climbed on top of him. She lifted her skirt up unbuckled his pants pulled out his dick. She slowly rubbed up on it until it was fully hard. She slid on top of super hard cock. He didn't feel like the same person that raped Aaliyah. She was enjoying fucking with him. She didn't give him the pleasure to come.

All of a sudden after she came, she could feel that his dick was starting to get limp. She knew that one of the medicines was kicking in and he wasn't shit. She got what she wanted. He can't do anything. He was helpless. Now it was my turn. I stepped in wipe that smile off my fucking face. I pulled out the syringe.

I stuck him in the neck with the syringe which laced with Epinephrine Hydrochloride and succinylcholine. The Epinephrine Hydrochloride was to keep his heart pumping and the succinylcholine was to allow his body to be paralyze while still feeling and seeing everything. I super glue his lids wide opened. Now, the fucker can't close his fucking eyes. I wanted to see every range of emotions, that he will show me.

"Tonight, it's about you.... Raymond." I put a tarp out on the floor and some carpet padding on top of the tarp to help soak up the blood. I'll tied that motherfucker to the chair. I made that his hands were hanging off and each leg was nicely tied to the legs of the chair. He couldn't move. His eyes was following me as begin to get prepare for this beautiful event.

He tried his hardest to move his lips, but he couldn't. He was paralyzed. He can hear everything and anything. But, he couldn't do shit. I ripped his clothes off with a pocket knife that I kept in my purse. I covered up with my best rain jacket and boots. I covered my hair with shower cap. I rolled out all instruments, they was to use on him. I put a trash can by the table. I got a cooler and put ice in it. I made sure he could see everything I was doing.

I pulled a chair up to him. "Before I even start I have a few confessions I must tell you. You are wondering why you are sitting here tied up butt ass naked in a chair. I don't you remember me. I use to be a super skinny kid. I was just starting to develop. I was dating your brother Damien. You decide to take me to an empty parking lot and rape me. When you were done, you treated me like trash. You laughed in my face and dropped my ass off at home. Still don't remember me?" He shook his head no.

My name is Aaliyah but you can call me Tasha. Aaliyah has multi personalities. I'm the evil one and today it's your lucky day. I have another confession your beautiful daughter Nadia. We've been good friends for months. Even more interesting she doesn't know our history. I have been gathering information about you and what you've done to her. So, this is revenge is not just for me it's for everyone you have abused and raped.

On a regular occasion, since your daughter is a lesbian and she loves me so much. I've allowed her to enjoy the pleasure of eating my pussy whenever she comes over. Tears was coming out of his eyes. Then his face was turning red. He was piss. There wasn't a damn thing he could do about it. The color of his skin begin to turn pale, when finally realized who the fuck I was. It was priceless!

Now, it's time for me to go to work. I love that I could see that he wanted to get up and fuck me up. There was nothing he can do! His ass was mine. I'm going to have so much fun! I'm enjoy every bit of. I'm going to have the footage to enjoy watching it over and over.

I went to work. I wanted to take my time. I commenced front top to bottom of him. I grab a pair mouth gag of to his mouth open. I took some forceps to pull and hold his tongue. With a scalpel, I slowly cut it off. Then, I threw in the cooler. The tears was rolling down his face, I cut his ears and nose. I stopped just giving him enough time to take this all in. I took mouth gag out of his mouth. I grabbed the pliers and pulled off each fingernail. I snipped off his fingers one by one with wire cutters.

I took the father's machete and waved in his face. I was making all these noise and all I could do was smile. I looked down and noticed that he piss himself. Fucking nasty ass bastards. It was okay, because I wasn't done. In one swing, I cut off his hands. I cauterizing his stubs with a hot iron, so he won't bleed everywhere. I then did the same thing to his feet. I slashing him up and down his body. I rubbed salt and lemon juice in each and every cut.

"What should I do next?" as I laughed in his face. I think I should do something with his dick. I went to Shit, he wasn't big enough for me to use the machete on. I took a regular kitchen knife and cut his dick and balls off cut. I was even nice enough to stitch up the area, so the fucker wouldn't bleed all over the damn house. I cut up his genitals into tiny little pieces and shove it down his fucking throat. He had tears pouring out his eyes. I was enjoying looking into his eyes. I could see the thrill in them. It was arousing.

I made him swallow every tiny little piece of his cock with bleach and then stapled his fucking mouth shut. Ensuring that he couldn't throw it up. Nowhere to go but out his nose. Oh my gosh, it was priceless. He was bleeding from every fucking part of his body. I have never seen so much blood. It was so exciting.

I untied him from chair and kicked the chair over. I was able to drag his body into the plastic drums. I sat the drum up. Then with some special gloves, I slowly poured fluoroantimonic acid over him. His eyes was rolling into the back of head. It really didn't care, I just know he better not die before I'm finish with him. I was a bitch, I took my time and slowly pouring in a ⅓ of the acid in the drum every 30 minutes until his body submerged in it. Tears were pouring out of his eyes. I make sure he was alive long enough to feel the pain.

I felt no pity for him. It took hours and a lot of patience with a glass of wine, I watched as everything that remind me of him was gone. I couldn't help, but to watch. Josephine and I sat there in the dining room watching him, as the acid ate him away. I sat back and enjoyed my masterpiece. Josephine was loving it so much that, she sat there and masturbate it to his death.

It was such a fucking rush for her. I cleaned everything up.

I was able to get the drum outside to push it down into the hole. I put all the dirty and covered it. The place was spotless. I stopped and took a deep breath, I smiled and closed the door behind me. I made sure I took my freshly cleaned tools and my cameras. I headed to PA. Even was nice to let Aaliyah out. Once, we were out of the area.

Aaliyah

I have no idea what happened today. I find myself in my car. I have no idea where I was coming from. I did have a note on the dash board to go to my family's house. So I head there. This black outs were happening more and more. I really don't know how my day went. I don't care either, I just know I feel different. I actually feel great! I went home and took a bubble bath. Which I haven't taken one such a long ass time. It felt good rolling around in my sheets. Laying in my bed surrounded by the darkness, for once, the night was silent.

The voices were quiet in my head. As the fan was blowing on me, crawling up with my pillows, with a smile on my face. I slept in peace knowing that I was in good mood. It's the first night, I slept like a baby.

Tasha

The fucked up part is that Aaliyah would never known what happened not unless we tell her. But the bitch is such a baby. She would ruin everything. It was best to keep that way. We woke to start a new day. We let Aaliyah stay asleep, so we could hide everything. I couldn't watch the video until later. I had to continue on acting normal. Even made an appearance in PA, to meet the family. I made sure I didn't skip a beat. I returned early from my trip to hang out with Nadia.

Chapter Ten

Returning back to school

I went back into my routine. I went back to school that rumors started up by the end of week that Coach Raymond had disappeared. I put on pretty damn good act. They had no leads and suspects. The had nothing to go on. It was as if he had vanish. It was funny, because his family didn't even take an interest in looking for him. A lot of his dirty laundry was coming out. The whole town find out about girls he rapped and abused. He was have swinger parties with the football team. He was supplying the team with drugs and alcohol. They find videos that was label with all his victims. Nadia was happy as hell. He never shows up for any of his hearings. Her mom was able to win all the courts hearings he missed.

By the end school year, the case was still going but the police had nothing. Nadia and her mother moved. Now that they whole town was blaming Nadia's mother for covering up for her missing husband. Even through her name was cleared people didn't care. They all felt sorry for Nadia, but the school were either her friend or assholes who teased her about being "touched by her father". I felt bad for her, but I hope everything gets better for her.

Maxwell

I thought I found someone I can trust and lose my virginity to instead he was an asshole he brought me over so he can have sex with me it was hard to even do anything with her couldn't get any privacy because I had to bring my brother's along his sister sitting around waiting to leave I remember sitting at his background and force my head down his dick I didn't know what I was doing I just put my head up and down on a stroke in motion that's the first time.

I never give head to a man. We tried really hard to get me to loosen up to have sex with my cousin finally we found some privacy and his parents garage on the bed making out and I couldn't do it I know he called me a fucking tease tell me get the hell pass his house cuz I still got to have strength to take off all my clothes and have sex with him two weeks later I guess he felt better that he can get me back he slept till my friends and a threesome I found that one of them blood all over your sheets. I was hurt

I had to get them back and I did it in the best way I knew. First, I got in touch with his best friend Tom Rouge and invited him over my house. I was so damn nervous have no idea why. I should have had Josephine do everything. But Josephine was freak and he didn't need know about her.

Tom had black, greasy hair slightly covers a lean, worried face. He had the most beautiful glittering blue eyes, set narrowly within their sockets, watch thoughtfully over the ladies He had soft skin gorgeously compliments his eyes and hair and leaves an intriguing memory of his past. This is the face of Mr. Tom, a true Utopian among humans. He stands common among others, despite his brawny frame. There's something bizarre about him, perhaps it's his unusual looks or perhaps it's simply a feeling of joy. But nonetheless, people tend to socialize with him, while helping him out in any way they can.

Trust me, he was like among the girl's in my school. I really didn't for him. He would do for I needed him for. I was wearing my choir school outfit. It was a black skirt and a white shirt. My cousin was upstairs watching TV. My brothers were walking about the house.

After chorus practice, Tom came over. I walked downstairs into the basement. We sat the couch He laid back on the couch and climbed on top of me. The pain that I felt when stuck his dick in me, hurt like a motherfucker. I wanted to cry. Damn his dick was bigger than Raymond. I controlled my emotions. Josephine was coaching me how to deal with it. Just then I started to feel the same sensation that I felt when Maya stuck her fingers in me.

After a few strokes, I was feeling better.

Fucking Tom felt so good. He was so big and it hurt but felt so amazing. This went on for about an hour or so. I heard giggling is above my head. I looked up and I can see in the cracks of the wooden floor. It was my brother. They were looking down at me as I was getting fucked by Tom. When he was done and he cum, he got up. That when noticed blood. He was amazed. He thought I was a virgin. I let him think that. My period decided to come early.

I thought it upon myself to make sure that it got back to Maxwell. Boy was he pissed. A week later Maxwell wanted to meet up. I agree to meet him at his house so we can "talk". I had other plans especially after what I did to Raymond.

I made my way over there by the end of week. Of course, I came with extra supplies. When, I got to his house, he let me in. He went to his room I was being a brat I went to the garage and waited for him. I had a different plan than him. I made sure planted my cameras before he came into the garage. He always kept a mattress in the garage, which I never asked. It was a little weird.

I didn't want it to his room. The idea sitting in his room, knowing that he had those bitches in there. Thoughts of what he did would interfere with my plans. I pull out the mattress and sat down on the bed. He finally made his way to the garage. He seemed a little annoyed, because he had to look for me. I didn't give two fucks either.

While, he sat there giving me this bullshit line about how he thought we were broken up. That it was had sex with my two friends, but I knew he was full of shit. Just a horny little fucking bastard he was. I wanted to grab the screwdriver off the nearby table and jab it in his fucking eye.

He stopped the conversation and excuse himself to the restroom. I reached in my purse, grab two pills, and drop them in his drink. He returned just in time as they dissolved. He slammed back the lace drink with no problem. As we talked within a couple of minutes, he started to pass out. Fucking lightweight! Oh fuck! I heard a car pulling the garage. I think it's mom. I quickly threw a blanket over of him.

Dammit I was hoping to kill him before anyone got home. I guess his mom will save the day. She returned quicker than it was excepted. I grabbed my shit, put my glass in the sink, and left my cameras there to record everything. I sneaked out the back door of his house. I return home and acted as if I never left the house. My family didn't know I had left. Late that night I decided to stop by Max's house. His father opened the door. There in the living room, there was rocking his mother was screaming and crying.

Josephine

With the best what the fuck," Oh my goodness? What's wrong, Mrs. Mary?

I acted as if I cared. I was even crying along with her. I had to think about not getting the chance to kill, which upset the most. As try to catch her breath between words, she explained to me how she came home. She was not aware that Maxwell was in the garage. She didn't know he was under a blanket and she killed him. She had ran over him.

I stay night and confronted the family and offer an helping hand. Maxwell's father seemed preoccupy with things dealing with his work. Personal he really didn't care for Maxwell. Him and Maxwell was always fighting. Which I could understand, because Mr. Charles wasn't Maxwell's father. Mr. Charles was leaving for weekend business trip and asked me to stop in, to check on Mrs. Mary.

Man, I should have won an Oscar for my performance.

I did as I was asked. I checked up on Mary. I actually needed to retrieve my camera. At least, I stayed to console her and explain to her it was an accident. She didn't know. Once she was good for the day, I retrieved my cameras.

I went home with my cameras. I ran straight to my room. I locked myself and hooked the cameras up to my computer. I watched it over and over. The blanket was barely covering his head. He was still sleeping. It a few minutes after I left, you can his mother backing up her car into the garage slowly. Of course, he never responded to the car. The car started to roll up his legs across his torso start crushing every bone along the way.

When the reached his head, I can see the tire resting on his head and blood oozing everywhere. I had to rewind it several times and zoomed in as well. I would love to be a fly in that room right then and there. I watched the video so many times as if it was the first time. It was priceless! Yeah, I got my rocks off. I think I masturbated 10 times before I finally decide to hide it in a little cubby hole in my room. I kind of felt bad for Mary, to lose her son like that. But oh well shit happens.

The Family

It wasn't long before shit started up in our house. Things wasn't the same anymore. We were at each other's throats. We never knew how the day was going to be from one day to the next. Aaliyah was able to be back in control for the most part. The family seemed like we're turning against each other. We were always fighting with one another. Terrell's fucking crazy ass threw a butcher's knife at me during one our fights. It had just missed me. I moved and it just caught into a nearby cabinet. I already knew he was fucking crazy, but he didn't know I worst. I did everything I could to keep me being the evil bitch out of me.

The relationship between my brothers and I was becoming very distant. We were starting to go our separate ways. I was kind happy because there was so many demons in our heads. I really didn't want to hurt them. Maybe, it was for the best. We weren't allowed to talk about those kind of feelings or what was going in our home. My cousin and my grandma were old school. They didn't like people in their business, but my cousin Phyllisa was forever looking for a pity party.

After, a fight between my brother and my grandma then it was my cousin and my grandma. Each of them grew apart and stopped talking to each other. My grandma ended up moving out. She found a place of our own far away from my cousin.

My hatred for my cousin was getting worst. She was becoming more and more lazy. She bought a small refrigerator for her room. She was at the point she was buying food and hiding in her refrigerator and her closet. She made sure to threat us about going into her room and the consequence, if we get catch.

Some days, we were hungry. We could only make tomato spinach soup. We were not to touch some the food that was in the kitchen. There was a small section of food that were allow to have. There were days, we went into her room and some of her food. But we were careless not to go crazy, because she would noticed.

I was learning how to control my personalities and hunger each day. I missed my grandmom, I was still able to visit her. I just had to go over to her house to see her when I was in the area. I was fine with that. Things just didn't feel the same, but it was nice not hearing my cousin and brothers fight with her.

The house started to feel empty. My brothers were going through different transformations. We were becoming more isolated. Growing up with this toxic family can be a profoundly isolating experience. This cocoon of home life has remain hidden for a long time, but people were starting to notice.

Terrell

Terrell was lashing out for all the shit that he couldn't deal with. The more Terrell act out, the more my cousin's patience is running thin. Terrell was stealing stuff, breaking and entering into homes and business especially after hours. He was mad all the time. He was a ticking bomb. At a drop of a dime, he snap off for no reason. When it came to my cousin, they were fighting more and more. Something happen between them two. He won't talk to anyone about it.

My cousin got sick of Terrell breaking the law and the police showing up all the time. She had him put in foster care with the state joint custody. Aaliyah didn't understand what was going on. She went into a really bad depression. Josephine and I took a knee. Jada took over. She was keeping all balance.

Terrell and I still was about to talk. He was diagnosed to him be bipolar, but I all ready knew that. We were all fucked up in the head. We are still a family. I missed him dearly. I was sobbing at night crying. Getting to talk him calmed me down some nights. Knowing he was okay, made it easy for me to sleep at night.

Almost a year later, Terrell was transferred to another group home. He was put on suicide watch. He had slit his wrist. It was breaking my heart. This won't have happened if our parents were still around.

Jay

Jay wasn't any better than Terrell. Jay would disappear after school. We would never know where or what he was doing. One evening, he burst into the house. This is when Jada jumped we didn't know much about her, but he more a mother to my brothers than anyone else. For now she only show up when it comes to her brothers. He was throwing up blood. Everything that was in my stomach was shooting out. As soon as he opened his mouth, more vomit flew out his mouth. It was terrified to see my brother like this. Jada didn't know what to do. She had no choice, but to stay with him. Of course, my cousin wasn't happy. We had a learner's permit, so we had to ask our cousin to take us to the hospital. Jay finally told me what happened. He was trying to commit suicide.

He was in tears. Jada was the strong for everyone. Jada was just keep him calm. Jada held his hand. My cousin finally bought her fat ass. She made sure sat by the vending machine. She kept her in the waiting room crocheting. She didn't bother to come in the back to check on my brother. Her day is coming soon. I had to watch them pour charcoal down Jay's throat.

Once they pumped his stomach. They admitted my brother in the psych ward. My cousin made sure she had shared custody with the state. Once Jay was well they transfer him my brother into foster care. After that incident, I didn't get to see my brother as much anymore. He came home on the weekends, but my cousin didn't even want to be bother with driving back and forth. I had to wait for phone calls to talk to my brother. Jada was great with Terrell and Jay, but she was hurting from the separation. They kept moving them to different homes. It was hurt keeping up with them. Jada did everything she could do for her brothers. I was now alone in this house with my cousin. The rage in me was building up more as my family was falling apart. My cousin had agree to keep us together. Now we were teens in high school. I saw less of my brothers. It was lonely in the house. At least they didn't have to deal with our cousin much anymore.

After the storm calm down with my brother, my cousin was getting out more. It must be nice. I love how she was keep partial custody of my brothers. She did that so she could still have control over them and any money they were getting. Phyllisa was happier these days. She actually was taking showers more. Thank God now we didn't have to smell her nasty ass. She was buying fancier clothes. She even had makeup on. She looked like a fucking clown. I didn't dare to tell her. That's her fucking problem.

Chapter Eleven

Miles, Phyllisa, and Aaliyah

Now we find out for all the new changes. Phyllisa had been dating a guy she met at the gym and now he was fucking moving in. This was going to be interesting. If she met him at the gym, he was probably in good shape. She wouldn't give me much details about him just that his name was Miles and he was 46, but that was it. I tried to easy drop when she was on the phone with one of her friends. She was talking and giggling quietly, so she couldn't be heard.

She was definitely in a good mood, so we knew what that meant.

One night, as I was making dinner for my brother and me when there was a knock at the door. Next minute, I know Phyllisa was running down the stairs. Phyllisa went to answer it. That was interesting, because she rarely even came downstairs even if it was for her. I followed behind her to be nosy. Before she answered the door, She straightened out her outfit and put on her famous fake ass smile. It was Miles.

I smiled back, and got my first proper chance to check him out. He wore a tight dark t-shirt with a simple pair of jeans and a leather jacket. The t-shirt showed off his obvious muscle, and I wondered briefly how he could stay in such great shape? But then he would have to be in shape to handle my cousin.

His dark hair was graying a little bit. It was trimmed very short. His day old stubble gave him a rugged look, but what made him really stand out though were his piercing eyes. His intense stare seemed to bore straight through me and his powerful eyes never left mine. A shiver of discomfort swept through me and as his gaze became too intensive and I averted my eyes.

I tried to pull my hand away from his unyielding, masculine grip, but he held onto it for a fraction longer than was comfortable, before eventually relenting. I brushed a strand of hair from my face, suddenly very self-conscious.

As, I sat down on the sofa and he took the armchair, his stare continued to pierce me. His obvious confidence and arrogance exuded from him. I felt very uncomfortable at his intensive and intimidating presence and tried desperately not to meet his eyes.

We sat in silence for a while, the quietness felt awkward and uneasy to me, but he seemed to be enjoying every second of it. Every time, I clumsily glanced up at him, his eyes were always on me, a slight smirk fixed on his face. A few times, I saw him checking me out and a hot blush spread across my face.

He made no attempt to talk to me or get to know me, no further attempt at any conversation. The longer his penetrating stares continued the more uncomfortable I got and the longer

I prayed that cousin would hurry up and take this fool to her room. I felt very exposed in my own home.

He hurried out to the garage as Miles slowly rose to his feet, he held his hand out in a wide grin. "It was nice meeting you." I did not want to take that hand. I did not want to feel his skin touching mine. However it would have been rude not to and I know my cousin would slapped me across my face if I was rude.

As, I hesitatingly took his hand. He tightened his grip around my hand, almost squeezing the life out of it. He pulled his arm back towards himself, forcing me to come closer to him and, with his free left hand. He wrapped it around the small of my back. His left arm forced me to press tight against him and panic suddenly swept through me.

I was close enough to smell his aftershave and faint linger of manly sweat, his arm had forced me tight against his crotch. I shuddered in disgust as his head lean in towards me to give me a kiss on the cheek. The motions of his head felt like he was going to give me a friendly granny like peck, but his head extended further back.

While giving me a deeper intake of his intoxicating odors. I wanted to fucking throw up all over him. Maybe that would improve his BO. Repulsion swept through me and I felt extremely weak as his stubble scratched along my cheek. His lips gave a lingering kiss near my ear and temple.

He finally released me and walked away. I stood in shock at his behavior. My cousin's car started and pulled away. As soon as, I knew he was gone I sat down on the sofa. A slight tremble came over me at the thought of the deeds the man my cousin was so in to had done. I could not believe that this was the guy my cousin was raving about so much. I trembled in disgust at the thought of his sexually over kiss and lecherous actions.

This motherfucker

I always felt so uncomfortable in his presence and now I was not going to have any respite from that uneasy feeling. Phyllisa did seem to hint at me for weeks that it was him pushing for him to move in together. At the same time Phyllisa was full of shit. I knew she wanted him to move in. Great this should be fucking interesting. As far as, I could tell he had some dirty little feelings that he wanted to get out of and moving in with us.

She loved it though, she reasoned that it made a change that the man was making the commitment and the running rather than the women. I resented Miles for moving in and I resented my cousin for letting him into our home. If I even dare to say something because she probably kick me out, too.

He completed the move just before Easter break. I visited my cousins in Philly, just so I could a break from my house. It was enough time for him to get comfortable and settled. In just a short space of time, he had made himself at home and I was very disconcerted that I felt an outsider in the place I grew up in.

Every time, I walked in on him and Phyllisa they were giggling away. Both of them we are having the time of their lives. They would pay absolutely no attention to me, and that was probably the best of it. I wanted to be the center of attention. I wanted my cousin to look after me as she used to. Now she looked after him and I was a distraction but would prefer to see her happy more than anything. The great part she wasn't taking her anger out on me for now.

Miles for the most part left me alone, which I was greatly relieved about. I would catch him checking me out and looking me up and down with unfriendly eyes, but I kinda got used to that. In fact the occasions he was completely wrapped up with Phyllisa. A feeling of envy came across me.

I wished that they were paying me attention. It kind of felt weird because cousin was home more. She even try bonding with my brothers and me when Miles was at work or hanging out with his family or his boys. She gave two fucks about us when Mile's boys were over. It was sickening. Suddenly I understood the saying, "Three's a crowd."

Each time, I saw him he would never say much. He would always make me feel uncomfortable. It always felt like he was checking out his girlfriend's niece. He always gave the impression that he did not care that I caught him doing it. Once, I felt his hand brush against the soft cheeks of my ass, as I turned to confront him he already walked away, probably feigning ignorance. Jada wasn't comfortable, she took a knee and like Aaliyah. We stayed dormant, for now. Our emotions were all over the map. We have hard time with all the changes. Aaliyah was actually great with being a good little girl.

Miles for the most part left me alone, which I was greatly relieved about. I would catch him checking me out and looking me up and down with unfriendly eyes, but I kinda got used to that. In fact the occasions he was completely wrapped up with Phyllisa. A feeling of envy came across me.

Weird Ass Night

My cousin wasn't home when I got there, which wasn't a big surprise. I was still feeling sick so I headed to my room, stripped down to my bra and panties and slipped under the covers. Then I remembered that I forget to bring up my clean laundry and do a load of dirty clothes from downstairs.

Dammit! I got up and went down the two flights of stairs to the basement. I started my load and then trudged back upstairs to my room and back into bed. I must have fallen asleep, because I woke when I heard the garage door opening. It was dark out. I looked at the clock and it said 1:30am. That seemed out of place for my cousin, but so be it. I peeked out the window and saw a car in the driveway with a man standing next to it. Of course it was mysterious Miles. I saw my cousin walked out of the garage. She was staggering a bit and it was obvious a little drunk behind her control.

Then, I watched as she threw her arms around him and began to kiss him passionately. Instinctively I backed away from the window, although I continued to peak around the edge of my blinds. Miles's arms were wrapped around her waist holding her up. I was shocked when she took her left hand and grabbed his right wrist. She then guided his hand under her short skirt. It was as if she was masturbating herself using his hand in the open view of our driveway.

Was this really my cousin I was watching? I really wasn't surprised about her behavior.

After about 30 seconds or so she pulled his hand back out from under her skirt and began to suck his index finger. Damn, It's not something I wanted to know about my cousin. My cousin was definitely more sexual than I thought. She then turned and pulled him toward the garage. I heard the door begin to close.

I began to panic a bit. My room was above hers and really didn't want to be home for this. I had a pretty good idea what my cousin had planned for him and I wasn't about to spoil that. I lay back down on my bed and pulled my blanket over my head. She would give me hell if I caused any problems especially when she is fucking intoxicated.

Sound travels pretty well between our walls. Every so often, they would quiet down for a couple of minutes and then the expletives would start again. I wasn't sure what was happening during those quiet times but once I did hear him say "That's right baby. Suck my dick like the slut you were born to be." After that I had a pretty good idea what was going on. I really didn't want to deal with this or hear it. I let Josephine have this one.

I have not seen a lot of porno, but I knew what "On your knees," followed by a moan meant. I guess he was human after all and eventually needed to cum. I tried to guess how much cum he must have sprayed on my cousin based on the number of times he groaned. It was hardly scientific, but my mind was so focused on what was happening in her bedroom that's what I thought about.

"You look like a glazed donuts," I heard him say. What a bastard I thought. It's bad enough you gave her a facial but don't mock her with it. "Thanks Sir," I heard cousin reply. "I love your cum."

What?!? She likes it? There was so much I didn't know about my cousin.

"Go to sleep now baby," he told her in a soothing voice. "Let it dry on your face and I'll call you tomorrow."

I didn't hear another sound from my cousin or Miles. I was clear he had fucked all the energy out of her. She'd probably sleep until noon. I began to relax thinking I would probably sleep until noon as well. Hopefully they were asleep because I needed to go to the kitchen and stole my cousin's wine coolers. Before heading downstairs I rolled the empty one in cousin's room. Yes I'm a bitch like that.

Oh shit

I went to the kitchen I suddenly started sweating a little bit more as I fretted over my options. I realized that I was horny and need a drink. I grabbed what I could carry. I then bolted up the stairs and into the safety of my bedroom. Just then I saw the amber of Miles cigarettes in the corner of my eyes. Miles stepped out the shadow. I didn't even realize that he was down there. As my thoughts raced I had a brief moment to watch the ongoing movie that I wanted to watch in my room.

Again, I made an attempt to leave and walk pass Miles, but he wasn't trying to let me pass. I said in a polite way, "I really should be going to bed, Miles."

"I know you would, but at the same time. I couldn't help, but notice that you have your cousin's wine coolers your hand and I'm pretty sure she wouldn't be happy if she found out that were drinking her wine coolers."

The fucked-up part that he was absolutely right, my cousin would have fucking lit into me. I threw the empty bottles in her room, while she was sleeping when I would drink up her wine coolers. I didn't tell him that.

"You might as well go ahead and drink them I won't tell! It will be our little secret." he stood there with an evil grin on his face.

I don't know his fucking plan was but I also knew that if I didn't go along with it. He would make my life a living hell with my cousin. Living with her was already enough as it is.

Feeling guilty, I took a swig and thought, I'll finish all the wine coolers off quickly. I wanted to bed afterwards. Miles grabbed a beer from the refrigerator. Miles pushed me to the living. I sat on the couch and Miles turned on the TV. He sat in the recliner. He just sat there staring at me.

Instead of sitting back onto the couch watching this boring ass chick flick with Miles.

I wanted to run to my room. I really didn't trust Miles. I also knew I had to get along with Miles. He was the type of bastard to make my life even harder. Miles came over by me and sat dangerously close next to me on the sofa.

His left hand held his beer shamefacedly near his crotch, the other arm stretched around the back of the sofa. I sat perched on the end of the sofa, unable to sit comfortably knowing that his arm was just behind me. I tried to stretch my nightie as far down my legs as they would go, they barely covered my thighs.

I was aware of his intense stare as my lips went around the bottle to take in as large a gulp as possible. I tried to ignore his leery eyes as I concentrated on the TV.

He placed his hand on my knee then up my inner thigh, and slowly started stroking upwards, all I could do was respond. I was torned I wanted it but I could feel Tasha wanting to kill him. I knew Tasha wasn't going to approve of this, but my needs were greater than hers. It felt weird I grabbed on my ear, just then Aaliyah stepped in but she wasn't aware of all of us. I know it was wrong, but Aaliyah was a pussy and was easier to go along with almost anything. She was a good little girl like that.

Aaliyah/Josephine

I really have no idea was going on. I didn't want to sound crazy, so I kept my mouth shut. I wanted to close my eyes and hope this was a nightmare. There was so many mixed emotions running through me I felt this feeling before, but I couldn't put my finger on it. For a brief few moments, I sighed in content as his strong hand stroked gradually up and down my inner thigh. It was only after the hand started to reach higher, up beyond my nightie, that I became fully aware and realized that it was Mile's hand I was responding to.

I kept my eyes shut. I was scared instead of being in delight, I shivered, mainly in revulsion at the thought of his hands touching me so callously, but slightly at what he was doing for me. As my mind raced and wondered how I'd got into this stupid situation and how I was supposed to get out of this, his hands started wondering even higher.

As his hands got closer and closer to my pussy, the more and more I did not want him to stop. As he made his strokes, I unwillingly arched my hips forward, exposing more and more of my thighs to him and giving him more and more access. I started rubbing my ear.

Oh wow that was a close one, I came back. Lord I have no idea what Aaliyah would have done. I don't know if Aaliyah is getting stronger or Tasha and I was slipping. We couldn't let Aaliyah know just yet.

Well anyway, his hot breath and the strong smell of beer washed over me as he leaned to my ear and whispered, "You are sooo beautiful."

I continued to melt as one hand continued to stroke my thigh and the other wrapped tightly around my shoulder. He started to nibble on my ear.

"I can't do this," I pleaded to him, "What about my cousin?"

"Shhhhh, don't worry baby."

Before I knew it, I felt his rock hard stubble

against my soft neck, my head lean to one side to open it up to him.

"I've wanted you from the first moment I saw you." he whispers.

I pleaded again, halfheartedly, "We shouldn't be doing this, what happens if someone comes down?"

"Shhhhh, just enjoy."

His hand was continued to stroke slowly and surely towards my pussy. No man had touched me as completely as Miles had, no man ever made me feel the way that he was. Of course I had boys roughly and coarsely grope me down there, but Miles knew what he was doing, he was turning me on.

Then something snapped. As his hand finally went beyond my thigh and he slipped a finger into me, I thought only of the fact that his finger had done similar things many, many times, not least with fucking cousin. I had disgusted myself again by allowing me to be manipulated by him. This man was living with us and know he was here fingering me.

All I can think to myself is what the fuck is wrong with me the thrill Revenge stuck in my head. I suddenly sobered up and fled the room and cried myself to sleep at my treachery.

The Guilt/Aaliyah

After that night, my hatred and fear of Miles increased. Every time I was alone with him I would feel incredibly intimidated. I told him he did that to me once, I wanted him to stop what he was doing, he just laughed in my face. Laughed with an arrogant, smirking, snugger.

He came over to the sofa where I was sitting and leaned into me, enveloping me. I shrank back further as his lips tickled my ear as he whispered to me; "You should be intimidated by me". He stood over me with unsmiling intent eyes as he broke into a smirk again and said, "I'm only joking, you should have more confidence in yourself".

Over the next few weeks that followed I felt incredibly uncomfortable around him. If we were in a room together alone, he would stare intently at me. More than once it got unbearable and I would have to leave the room to the sanctuary of my bedroom, I spent more and more time around Josie's.

He would make it obvious in checking me out, his leery eyes all over me. And once, when I made the mistake of wearing a low cut top, I eventually noticed he had maneuvered himself to get a glimpse down it.

Phyllisa was too oblivious to notice him gawking at my breasts. I felt so vulnerable and alone, she was too wrapped up in him to perceive his obvious wondering eye and perversion. I was his girlfriend's niece for fucks sake!

His snidely and depraved comments started to get me down. It was just little digs here and there, but they were demoralizing. Little digs about me, sometimes he would make derogatory comments about the clothes I would wear, other times he would comment on my perfect hair.

He once mockingly waved a $20 bill in my face, but only if I would give him a blow job. I almost slapped him for that, but he left a note on the table saying it was payment for allowing his fingers to taste my pussy.

Everything he did tired me out, I would have

to be on my guard whenever he was about. And if he did not do anything or say anything I would always be wary about what would happen the next time we bumped into each other.

Chapter Twelve

His exploitation of me did not stop at his ogling or his words, his hands started to wonder and I found myself more and more often fighting his hands. He would pat my knee and leave his hand a fraction too long, he would stroke my hair, slap my bum, anything as long as it meant getting his hands on me, touching and groping me.

He would not even be subtle about it, he would do it blatantly in front of my cousin. Once, when I was wearing a crop top and tracksuit bottoms, he crept up behind me, grabbed me in a pincer by my naked waist and started tickling me. His obvious hard-on thrust into my bum as I tried to escape. We both fell to the floor, and my cousin, who was in the room, was simply in tears of laughter.

Out of her sight, quick as a flash he managed to slip his large hand down the back of my sweatpants, down the back of my panties and around my bum. As he quickly withdrew his hand and got up, his middle finger slid tauntingly across my asshole. As I rose up, I was almost in hysterics as Miles leered and laughed at me, and my cousin oblivious to the fact that her cousin had just been sexually assaulted. Absolutely humiliated, I fled the room close to tears.

I did once try to hint to my cousin about his ways, but she just snorted it off and said he was being affectionate. She shrugged it off and called me a liar. She said I need get along with him and stop making up stories.

I was never going to forgive him for what he finally did to be. Nor was I going to forgive my cousin, because she really didn't care what he did to me. He caught me at a very vulnerable moment, a moment of weakness. I was low, so depressed, and he came and took advantage. He came and said the right things, with his smarmy charm, his aggressive and macho behavior, he cajoled his way to what he was looking for me.

Towards the end of Summer, I received my exam results and they were not good. I needed to get my GPA up better, if I wanted to get into a really good college. I was devastated and so disappointed. I was not expecting to do badly, I honestly thought I had done well. My cousin was on my ass. She kept saying things such as I was not putting enough effort in and she had sacrificed everything for me to have a good education.

She made me feel really guilty, made me feel worse than I already did. The devastation and disappointment of failure was added to by my friends' results and my cousin's reaction.

My cousin had never been like this before, she had always been supportive and encouraging. But this time she was very angry and upset, and she upset me so badly. The one time I really needed her and she flew right off the handle, and completely over-reacted. I had no doubt it was Mile's influence.

For once, maybe not intentionally, but now that my cousin had a boyfriend. He was more important to her than I was. I was just a distraction during the holidays, her real fun was with the hunk who shared her bed. That's what it seemed to me anyway.

My cousin decided that *"she"* needed cheering up, so she called a few of her friends and left for the afternoon and probably most of the evening. I knew what these trips were like, she would hit the mall and then for some drinks, not getting back until after she had emptied most of her bank account and most of the bar. She left me with the creep.

Josephine and Miles

Josephine had taken over now. Josephine knew what was coming. I moped around the front room, with a bar of chocolate, the TV and my misery as company. Even Josie had abandoned me, she was too busy celebrating her results. I did try and convince Tasha to come down and relax, but there was no way

I would have enjoyed it. In many ways I was disappointed Tasha did not try harder to cheer me up, or to come share in my misery.

Only Miles was there, only Miles made an effort. At the time I thought and felt it was because he genuinely cared for me, but eventually I realized it was just because he wanted to use me, use me in the most literal sense. I had to be one step ahead of him. I started hiding cameras around the house. I was able to activate them on my phone.

As, I started on my second bar of chocolate he came and stood in front of the TV. I started up the cameras, hoping he won't notice what I was doing. I huffed at him, "Will you get out of my way."

He just stood there staring intently at me, I ignored him and pretended that I could see through him. As always his tight t-shirt clung to him.

"Are you going to be a child forever, going to mope around like a six year old?"

"Yes." I replied.

He deliberated for a moment before deciding on his course of action, he grabbed my arm and wrenched me from the sofa. He started pulling me towards the kitchen.

"Oww, you're hurting me. What are you doing?"

My heart started pounding at the force of his grip and the thought of his masterful control over me. Despite trying to pull away from him I did not have the strength to fight him.

"We're getting you drunk, then you can stop this silly behavior."

He hauled me into the kitchen and then pulled out a chair for me, he pushed me roughly onto it and looked long and hard at me. I tried to meet his eyes, eyes that no longer seemed to be leering but penetrating me deeply. I still could not do it, he had such an overpowering look.

He walked over to a couple of cupboards and pulled out a bottle of vodka and a two glasses, it was evident that he was going to be drinking as well. He poured out two generous helpings into the glasses and handed me one. I took it and swished the liquid nervously.

"Go on, all in one. It'll do you some good."

I watched as he took one gulp of the clear drink, his face contoured as it went straight down. I swished and stared at the glass again.

Everything sensible in me screamed and said no, do not have that drink.

Do not drink with the devil! This man who has touched you. This man who has manipulated me, Miles who leers and gropes at me. This same asshole who despite all his perverted ways and advancing age is still very alluring, the man who is my cousin's boyfriend. I could smell the bullshit seeping out of his pores. If he only knew what demons that lived inside of me. I am pretty sure, he would think twice about fucking with me.

It was the thought of drinking with my cousin's good looking piece of shit boyfriend, that lit a match. Tasha knew exactly what I was doing. I was going for "please, don't bullshit!" I wanted to take advance and exposed this motherfucker the best I way I could. I wanted to payback for the cruel words and lack of support from my cousin. I wanted to hurt her for the hurt, the pain she had inflicted. That bitch didn't gave a shit about us. I was more interested in Miles, then she was in my family.

Drinking with him seemed an ideal way to do it. I tried to ignore the times he had humiliated me, the times he made me feel so small. But now he was making me feel nice.

He was paying me attention and making me feel better about myself and making my cousin seem so small and insignificant.

In a quick move, he dove on top of me and dragged me completely onto the bed, He pinned my arms pinned down and I tried to keep my legs shut but within a second he had forced them open and was lying on top of me. His huge cock stood at the entrance of my pussy. I tried to fight him and struggle, but he was far too strong, I felt helpless and trapped as he sneered at me.

"Get off of me."

"I haven't finished with you yet. You've had your deserts but my cock wants a taste of that sweet young pussy.

Anger rose in me, "Get off me you fucking bastard. I don't want this anymore."

"Ohhh, a little feistiness. I was wondering when you were going to show that."

He was loving this, he was in total control. He had me trapped, my arms pinned down by his strong hands, the weight of his huge body over me. I felt so helpless, so powerless. His face inches away from me, the strong reek of alcohol nauseated me, and I suddenly realized his body stank of a mixture of mine and his sweat.

His cock was at my entrance, he was going to fuck me whether I liked it or not.

Don't lie about not wanting this, your pussy is *so* wet."

Before I knew it he had plunged his huge cock into my dripping pussy. I yelped in a mixture of shock and pleasure at how deep he forced himself into me. I bit my lower lip and grimaced in pain at how far in his cock was reaching. I tried to focus on the short sharp rhythm he was building up and tried to block out the pain. It felt like he was ripping me in two.

As he continued to ram his dick into me. He made the situation a whole lot worse. "Did you know your cousin loves anal. She's such a fucking slut. I used to love taking her up the ass. Don't like it anymore, my dick slips right in. That's why I went for your young sweat ass of a cousin."

A slow sneer came across him as he said, "All the sex with none of the wrinkles."

"You fucking bastard, let me go NOW!" I was so upset, almost in tears. I was being fucked by a bastard and there was nothing I could do.

He lay on me for a moment before wearily

getting up. His warm cum started to freak me out. He stood up and searched out for a towel.

He stood over me angry, "Next time I don't want you to make such a big deal. It's just sex for fucks sake. Keep your mouth shut and don't tell your cousin. Even if you tell your cousin, she isn't going to believe you anyway."

"Next time? There was no way there was ever going to be a next time. He threw a towel at me and told me to wipe myself. To be honest, I really wanted and it came me something over his head. I liked fucking but wanted to crush his dreams. He wasn't going to last long in this house. I will have the last word. I really should become an actress. I was getting better. Tasha and I are becoming the perfect team.

I started crying as he fixed himself. I kept playing the role until I heard him walk right of the house. I rubbed my ear. Just like that Tasha was back. Tasha and gathered all the data from the camera and put together on a CD. Put together a plan to kill him off. Afterwards, we took a shower and we went to bed as if nothing happened.

A month later/Tasha

I was fucking ready for him. Over the last few weeks, I overheard him bragging about raping some girls. He boost about how young the girls were. I soon find out that he was in this secret club. The secret club was a sex club/ pedophile ring. I find out as much as I could about the sick and twisted the club was. I find out as much as I could about each and everyone, especially Miles. I commenced to keep a 4x5 size yellow notebook that with me at all times. It was personal notes and kill list of all sick bastards. I now had a plan to seek revenge and to still get my fix in.

Something in me just snapped. I was back and up to no good. After seeing what Josephine did to get us a new kill, was a blessing. Each kill wasn't as good as the first one, but the thrill was more exciting. Learning different ways to get to kill my victims. As much I wanted to keep acting innocent, that was boring. My thirst was getting stronger. Now, I wanted my cousin to feel the pain of losing someone she loved. I would love to kill her, but I wanted her to suffer.

It was just another Friday night but just like

any other. I knew Miles would be going to a bar in Camden. My cousin and I always had to pick him from the local police department from getting into bar fights or he was find passed out in back alley.

This Friday on June 13, 1997 was going to be a fun day for me. I had plans to sleep over at a close friends' that lived in Cherry Hill. Everything was set. Molly was this brown skinned girl. I had this unsociable feel about her. Molly and I really didn't hang out this much. She was 5' 6" tall. She had narrow shoulders and toned arms, a broad torso with defined muscles, and strong legs.

Her black hair was very short and thick. She had a demented and untidy personality. She has an oval face with a square jaw. Her eyebrows are neat, and her narrow, friendly eyes are light brown. Her nose is large and she has thin lips. She usually wears expensive clothes. Her particularly noticeable features are her cheap perfume, her white, sparkly teeth and her nice cologne. We talked here and there. I stayed in touch with people I knew would need later.

I knew that I would be able and sneak out and returned, because the whole family were heavy sleepers. I was able to steal a double-barreled, saw-off shotgun and a .22 rifle from my neighbor. My neighbor was this 87 year old man. He always allowed people and teenagers to hang out his house. He was the neighbor perv. I grabbed the gun and rifle after school without anyone knowing.

I went over my friend's house and hide the weapons under the bed I was going sleep in. We had movie night with her family. Just like that everyone went to bed at 11pm. I stole the mother's car keys. I had to be extra careful. I didn't need to lose my license before even getting it. I parked far away from the bar. With my backpack with the weapons, I made my way over to the bar at I find Mile's car, parked in the alley of the bar. I broke the lights in alleys near his car. I ciphered the gas out of his car, I let drain out into the alleyway. I got into position and hide next to dumpster where I had a perfect view of his car.

At 3am, there he was slowly walking to car, trying keeping him balance. He got in his car and of course it didn't start. He got out of his car.

He had dropped his keys. Perfect timing. Just he bend over to pick up his keys. I screamed out his name and beckoned him over. He actually came over. As soon as, he caught a glimpse of who I was. Before, he could say anything, I shot him in the face and stomach.

He died where he fell. I felt fucking free. His blood was so warm, when it splash back at me. As the blood poured out his body. I grabbed empty gas can out of his car. I collected his blood. I dismember his lifeless body right there. With all his organs spread out on the ground, it looked like a work art. I gave him a beautiful Glasgow smile. I castrated him. I was satisfy!

It was 5:30am I needed to head back. I grabbed everything and drive back to Molly's house. I got back just in time before everyone got up. I hide the can in the back of Molly's house. I called the old fart that I stole the gun and rifle from. I had him come and pick me up. I was able to grab the can and head home. I was able to return the gun and rifle before he notice that they were gone.

I went home. No one was there. I took the can of blood upstairs into the family bathroom. I locked the door, I set about to fill the claw tub with hot water. I got undress and stood in the water. I took the gas can and I poured the blood over my head. I felt so empowered. Feeling blood all over my naked body. I rubbed it all over myself. I enjoyed every bit of it. I sled in the hot water. The mixer was so fucking nice.

I went on with my day as if nothing happened. Later that day, my cousin returned early from work. She was crying. I had to put on my I "give two fucks" face on. I asking what was wrong. She told me about Miles. I acted surprise. I acted like I was heart broken.

Apparently, the cops lost a lot of evidence. A rookie was smoking and was told to put his cigarette out. The rookie dropped it on the ground in igniting the gas that no one even noticed. Everything and including Miles got caught on fire.

Chapter Thirteen

Aftermath

After the lose of Miles, things changed in our house. I knew things were going to change but I at the same time I didn't care. My cousin was crying and shamed. She Miles death was all over the news for days. She hated leaving the house. All his dirty secrets had been exposed. The neighbors and my cousin's friends learned about him raping underage teens, his drugs, and bites about what he did to me. Of course, I was the one leak his dirty out to the local newspaper. People spectacle that Miles was probably killed by someone seeking revenge. That was true, but they had no idea who. No evidence was find. If did have any evidence, it went with the fire.

My cousin started having tantrums more like meltdown. She was being criticized for being with him and how could she didn't the shit he was doing. My cousin was hiding more in her room. She was so depress.

She was bad. We were fighting almost everyday. She become even more evil and nasty. One day, I was listening to *Nine Inch Nails*. She hate me listening to metal. I really didn't care. She was so pissed that she came into room and ripped my radio out of the socket. She didn't approve of me listening to anything different that wasn't approved by her. I tried to defend why I was listening to NIN. She didn't want to hear it and punch me in the right side my head. I had 50% lose of my hearing in my right ear. I really wanted her to die. I prefer her to die alone and with a slow death.

I had to start to make some changes. I need to get my license and move the fuck out. I started looking for jobs I could make money quick. If I stayed here any longer I may exposed. I really need to keep learning how to control my hunger.

Driving License/Moving

It didn't take me long to get my license. I needed to get a car. As much I wanted to do it before moving out. but I couldn't take it anymore. I decided to move out on my own on announced. I packed up all my stuff secretly and stuck it in the basement. I moved in with a friend and their basement nearby so I can still stay close to my grandma. It was hard secretly about moving out, but her parents didn't knew the shit that I was going through.

I refuse to let people in my life. I still have 6 more months before I walk down with the rest of my class. In the meantime, I was going to get a job. I wanted to start building up something from nothing for myself. I know if I stay there any longer I would have killed the bitch. My brothers and grandmom were gone. This house haunted me with empty dreams and bad memories.

The Proud Bear

I looked for jobs closer in the area were I

lived. I found this one place in Westhampton. It was a little bit closer to my high school. It was a waitressing. The french owner was kinda cute, but he was married with kids and wasn't my type. He also was bumbag, always hitting all the waitress. He couldn't keep his hands to himself. I almost put a fork in fucking eye. I was able to stop myself.

He was little too old for me. I work like a dog every Tuesday. I was only way to waitress. I had to bus my own tables, and cash out the customers. I learned the meaning of hustling. A full restaurant to do to take care of. I worked on the weekends where we have split sections. Some days was great and others was a fucking nightmare. Shit, we let Aaliyah do all the work. She was perfect waitress. She couldn't the fucking boss being a fucking a pig the minute his wife and kids left the restaurant. Each day I dreamed about killing him and bathing in his blood.

One day, my cousin saw me walking to work. She actually was nice, but there was always a catch to her being nice. My cousin drop me off at work. Today just felt like an odd day to be at work and seeing my cousin. She even offer for me stay over the house to catch.

I had a bad feeling. I prayed for customers to come in to keep me busy. But no one came in that day not a single customer. Of course, my boss started drinking. I had hoped my boss will be nice and send me home early, but instead of my boss got pissed drunk. He decide, he want to try to rape me.

Aaliyah tried my best to stay away from him. I find things to keep me busy. He called me into his office. We were talking in the office that is when he pinned me in the corner. He tried to push up on me. I escaped out of the office. I didn't want to just leave my job. It would be consider as abandonment and instantly fired.

I did everything I could to stay away from him. I keep working until my cousin called me. I took the phone call in the back of the restaurant, hoping that he wouldn't follow me. The bitch called me to pick a hoagie from the *Wawa* that was next door. Aaliyah was so scared. Josephine and I tried to not step in, because we knew exactly was going to happen if we did. She tried to hint to her that she really need her to come pick her up. The bitch refused to come and get me. She just wanted a hoagie. Fuck her!

She couldn't even get Jose the dishwasher boy to help her. He was too busy in his own little world. Aaliyah was still on the phone, when her boss found her in the back of the restaurant. This motherfucker pulled a chair up behind me. He pulled me down on his lap. Aaliyah resisted his every move. Phyllisa was useless. Aaliyah was about have a panic attack. She started to rub her ear lobe. Well you know what that meant.

Josephine kicked in. Josephine hung up on her cousin. She flirted back but she didn't give into his passes. It was closing time. The dishwasher boy and myself finished closing the restaurant. I was able to convince Jose to give me a ride home. I didn't trust my boss especially if he saw me walking home.

Just as we thought we were done. The fucking drunk asshole decided he wanted to cook. I wasn't going to sit there and let this motherfucker take advance of Aaliyah. She's been taking a shit for men all these years and I couldn't take it anymore. Josephine and I knew what had to be done. I took over.

I was going to show my boss a whole different side. I had to plan something quick. I wanted the Jose to witness it. But I had to be careful. My boss was drunk and was trying to clean up the mess he made. I sat in the corner of the kitchen. I saw an opportunity.

Trying keep his balance, he knocked over a container of oil onto the floor. I couldn't even make this up if I try. I didn't say a word them. Jose ran to the utility room to get some cleaning supplies. I just sat there with my arms folded. As Jose was returning, my boss had a handful of knives in his hand. This was too perfect. I acted as if I cared, my boss was walking towards the oil mess.

In slowly motion, Jose and I yelled at my boss to stop, as we ran towards him. But we didn't get to him fast enough. He slipped on the oil. He turned to catch his balance but lost. Instead of throwing the knives away from him, he held on them tightly. It was beautiful, he had impaled himself. The knives went straight into his chin and neck. He catch his jugular vein. It was a perfect death. I was close enough to him, that blood had splash back at me. Oh my goodness it felt so good. I wanted play in his blood.

I had to play the terrifying part. We let Aaliyah out, she was amazing because she had no idea. Jose called 911. We were there for hours talking the police. The police even saw the harassment before his death. They find the recording of the whole incident. I am so glad I didn't put my hands on him. Officer William Hannity a well know officer in the town. He pulled me aside and apologize what for I went through. Aaliyah was traumatized. She was crying and begging to go home. He finally let us go. He even promised to talk to the school, to excuse me for a week off. I didn't feel sorry for him or for Aaliyah.

I was still nice. I got my cousin, her fucking hoagie. She offer for me to watch over the house while she was on vacation. I didn't bother to tell her what happen. Officer Hannity did it for me. She asked me to move back in. She was being to nice. I really didn't want to. But I was going to take advance of being back home.

A month later, I, well I mean Aaliyah started dating this guy from a high school rival. Jake with his chestnut, curly hair slightly covers a skinny, friendly face. He had sparkling gray eyes, set delicately within their sockets, watch enthusiastically over the rivers they've felt at home at for so long.

He had a scar that stretching from just under his left eyebrow. It ran towards the right side of his lips and ending on his left cheekbone leaves an aching memory of fortunate adventures. He stood high among others, despite his scraggy frame. There's something puzzling about him, perhaps it's his mysterious or perhaps it's simply a feeling of guilt. But nonetheless, people tend to brag about knowing him, while spreading rumors about him behind his back.

He was a outcast and a loner. He really didn't have much friends. I met him in my history class. We started hanging out after school, then on weekends. Well the rest is history.

After four months of dating, Jake grew distant. It got to the point that I was starting to worry what the fuck was up with him. Jake got worse when he got his Trans Am. He was showing signs that he was cheating on me, but I didn't proof. I really didn't want to look, because I probably would kill him. I left it alone for now.

Alcohol and New Chapter

The first experience of getting drunk was often quite carefully planned. Getting hold of alcohol is not straight forward for young people who are under age. The Crown Liquor Store and The Hot Mess Liquor Store initiatives that require shop and bar keepers to ask for proof of age for anyone who they think looks less than 21 or 25 make it difficult for young people to buy alcohol themselves.

Some young people persuaded older brothers and sisters to buy alcohol for them or find way to get a fake ID. There would kids hang around outside the shop and asking strangers to buy alcohol for them. They eventually got someone who would always agree. I was lucky because I stayed over my cousins when she was actually in a good mood. She was loaded with unlimited supply of all kinds of alcohol. Since Jake wasn't around much I started hanging out Bruce.

I was hanging out Bruce. Bruce was a childhood friend and the best friend of Jake. Bruce and Jake, I have been friends for years. When Bruce find out that I was dating Jake, he was happy for us. You could tell we both had a thing for each other but never dare to acted on it. We did the role playing game through the neighborhood.

An reenactment of our versions of a witch hunt. This is I got to come out and dress in all black with my knee high boots. I love hanging out Bruce. I actually forgot about Jake. Bruce was dating this girl named Molly. He didn't get to see Molly that much because she was always camping. She never invited Bruce. I told that was weird, but I kept my opinions to myself.

After months of hanging out, Bruce and I soon find out what was up with Jake and Molly. Jeff was fucking Bruce's girlfriend Molly. Both Bruce and I were hurt. We did our best not to talk about it. Since I had the house to myself, invited Bruce over. We watched *The Crow* and drinking all kinds of liquor from my cousin's closet. This is when I find out much I loved vodka and *Jack Daniel's* whiskey.

We watched the movie three times that

day. We made our way over to the local fire company where he worked. We met up with a few of our role playing friends to play some strip pole. I sucked I didn't play much but I was having great time until Molly showed up. I was hinting to Bruce about my feelings about him. Bruce never caught on. Josephine even came out, but Bruce fall for Molly's bullshit.

We ended the game early. I was devastated. I felt like shit. We made plans to meet tomorrow to confront Jake. I never told Bruce how I felt. I went home and crashed for the night. I didn't want to think about Molly and Jake.

The next morning, I woke up. Surprisingly I didn't have a hangover. I got ready to meet up Bruce and fucking Molly. I met up with Bruce, Molly, and we head over Jake's house. I sat in the backseat as I watch Molly and Bruce acting like nothing happen. With our luck, he was outside washing his car. We asked him questions about cheating on me.

Jake didn't care for us showing up unannounced and wasn't going to admit to cheating. He keep cleaning his car as if we wasn't there. Fuck this I walked up to him and hit him in the head with a rock. He dropped to the ground. He was crying like a little bitch. He told us everything.

There he was laying on the ground bleeding out. My eyes start glowing like a demon at the sight of his blood. He was stupid motherfucker. He though we would never find out about it. That was the last time I seen him. I moved out my cousin's house. I didn't tell anyone were I was going. I didn't tell Bruce either.

Chapter Fourteen

As I passed my driver's license. I disappeared to Florence New Jersey. I started looking for a car to get. I wanted something quick and good. I knew I was going to be doing a lot of driving. Therefore I needed something good millage. I was also looking for a place to move to. As much as I loved my friends I needed some privacy. I needed to be careful about letting the people around me learn about my secrets. I was hanging with my old classmates I grew up with. Many of them were the best kind of friends because we had are own little secrets but we didn't care to ask.

Stripping/ Josephine

Throughout the years, I have always wondered what a woman's motivation was for taking her clothes off for a living. Did they due out of desperation? Unlike Tasha, I knew how to work my body to get what I wanted. Tasha and I work together better than the others. My top priority was to grow up and become independent as soon as possible. To me, true independence meant never having to ask my family for money.

They were less than willing to provide it. It was a waste of time to even ask them. I love the fact that I could get things I wanted like a car for myself. I heard that strippers made good money. I did some math and figured that a girl could make some decent money, but I thought you had to be a gymnast or have dance background to be a stripper.

Living in New Jersey wasn't cheap either. My spare income wasn't nearly enough to survive on. If was going to survive, I had to stop working for piece shit unknown restaurants. I was driving me nuts. I felt so infantile and trapped. I was thinking about becoming a stripper. It couldn't be that bad. I'd always been a pretty repressed young woman with perfect grades, respectable hobbies, never so much as a parking ticket, but something about the idea of exotic dancing captivated my imagination.

I started look into becoming a exotic dancer. Just before my 19th birthday, I saw an ad for an "amateur night" contest at a local strip club. The amateur night was a few weeks away, so I slowly built up to it. I bought myself some 5-inch platform heels, then I practiced walking around my room, then I got myself a lacy lingerie set, then I picked out my set list *Rob Zombie "Living Dead Girl and Dragula"* I had three sets of play list depending on the day or the crowd of people. If it was all bikers I did my heavy metal songs and had my my R'n'B songs as well. Finally, the night of my big debut arrived.

I took my crazy ass friend Carmela with me for protection. She was an average size chick with the brightest red hair. She barely smile, but she never afraid to get her hands dirty. She was born and raised in a biker's family. Her family was well known out New Jersey. Her father was a 1% for the Hell's Angels. Despite her family's reputation, Carmela was a good person with a mean strike. She had her moments.

She was the person always wanted on your side. I have seen fight before she can be dirty at times. I remember one day in high school a girl kept fucking with her. They wanted to fight. Therefore, they meant Mill Dam park. Carmela ran up on the girl while the bitch was on the swing. With one swing with her aluminum bat, Carmela knocked the girl out.

Afterwards, she duct tape the girl to the merry go around nake with honey on her. The bees had a field day with her. That bitch had a big knot on the side of her face when she returned the next day to school. Carmela never got in trouble for the event. The girl and her family knew not to fuck Carmela or more shit was going to rain down on them.

She was always good to Aaliyah. They were close like sisters. She was not aware of us. We would never show her us. I probably would understand but the less she knew the better, we felt about her safety.

Carmela drove me to a place called *Illusions*

on Route 130 in Florence. It was a bright pink building that fall back off the highway. There was so many bikes outside. I was so nervous. I wanted to throw up. Before I went in I drink down a half bottle of Jack Daniel's before I grabbed my shit. Carmela and I came up with a safety word *Batmen*. I have no idea where that came from. I was hoping the alcohol would kick in.

Illusions was essentially a cozy neighborhood dive bar, but with naked ladies. Most of the customer were "regulars" or as they jokingly called themselves, "pathetic losers". The dancers were exceptionally diverse every ethnicity, body type and educational background was represented.

Unfortunately, the place was run by a mega-douche bag named Billy a red-faced, testosterone junkie who managed the club like an oppressive dictator. I quit after about a year, largely due to Billy's appalling behavior.

Standing backstage, I was completely terrified not because I was about to expose my body to a room full of strangers, but because I was convinced I would trip and fall! I was giving a stage name, "Spice". I stepped onto the stage. My songs came. But the moment I stepped onstage, I went into an altered state. I don't know what I was thinking. I guess I was waiting for the fear to hit me.

I stripped down to a red lace push-up bra that barely covered his nipples, black stockings and garters, a red lace thong. I struggling to balance on high heels, I said fuck it. I kicked them off. Then I was really into. All I could hear was the music. I did a few pole tricks. I wasn't even his body was it?Turns out, I was a total natural.

I won first place competing against several dancers who were far from "amateurs," I'll have you know and made $400 on the spot. The rush of adrenaline and exhilaration was indescribable. I knew, without a doubt, that my life was about to shift dramatically. Dancing made me feel like I am a star. Dancing is only degrading if you let it be.

What I really wasn't prepared for was the emotional aspect of having people touch and view my body like it was a commodity. I love that shit now, but that first couple shifts it was really interesting. It really took time for me to acknowledge and work past my initial shame and insecurities.

I started that night. Each night, I started approaching each male that was available and asking them if they wanted a dance. It felt like the first day of school. All the other dancers knew each other in the dressing room, but I kept to myself a bit. In just one week I earned enough money to get my first car. It wasn't the best car but it was best I could buy for now. It was old crown vic with a prince blue color. It was an old cop car but it was the best I could get last minute. Because winter was coming and the car I wanted wasn't good for the winter days in Jersey. Now that I was a stripping, I didn't tell anyone. But having a secret was hard but I really knew how people looked at people who were like me in this industry. Making myself financially stable felt was a big fucking rush. Being broke all the time was making me feel shit. Finally feeling like I had some money was empowering.

Shortly afterwards I was able to get myself a studio apartment in Burlington township. Which it was perfect, because it was between my family and my jobs. Once I got use to going and coming to work, Carmela went back to her side jobs. She was never to far, if I needed her help.

There were certain stereotypes about strippers I soon find out. They're all drug addicts, they're all skanky, and they're all single moms. I won't lie I met more than a few drug-addled slutty baby mommas here. I had to be careful who I called my friend. But I also met a few PhD students, professional tattoo artists, fashion models, real estate agents, event planners and hair stylists.

The happy, healthy dancers had three things in common, a day job, a savings plan with an exit strategy. But that didn't always go as plan. Some started on drugs, or some got so wrapped up int this life that never made to their goals. A few girls got fired as soon as I started and they ended up giving me the lunch time slot. It wasn't bad shift.

I find myself daydreaming about nothing in particular to pass the time of 12 minutes, when I was on the stage. I tell myself to smile. As a exotic dancer, we had to learn the proper strip club etiquette, much to my chagrin. There are some things about stripping that were difficult, especially how much your self-esteem becomes so attached to how much you earn on any given day. Go figure who would have though, we had to have training in proper etiquette.

I am filled with disdain for the customers who do not tip, but sit and watch and direct you to do things for no money. I think of how cheap these fuckers are, what bills I need to pay. I don't want them to touch me, but I am afraid they would say something violent if I tell him "no'.

I could only think about how bad these guys smell and try to hold my breath. I spent the dance hyper-vigilant to avoiding their hands, mouths, and crotches. I was glad we were allowed to place towels on the guys' laps, so it wasn't so bad.

I picked my customers pretty selectively, and they were all over the map in terms of income level, age and relationship status. They never knew my real name, but we forged deep connections that lasted weeks, months. I still keep in touch with one or two of them, believe it or not! Thanksgiving is always the best day to work in clubs because the people who are in there either A. have no family, or B. can't get home for whatever reason. So everyone goes in the club and gets wasted.

The majority of customers were really fun to talk to, which made working a desirable place to be. I didn't socialize with male customers after work. I damn sure wasn't going to put my job in jeopardy for them either. More importantly I didn't despise or belittle them. I could relate to their longing, their loneliness and their desire for female companionship, because I shared those feelings, too. Even knowing what I do, men hit on me constantly. It doesn't stop them in the least. With all the negative stereotypes, you'd think this wouldn't happen.

Men love everything about women. I've made money on days when my hair is half-done and I have no make-up on. I've had men come up to me after my stage set, when I was huffing and puffing from dancing and doing pole tricks, they would beg me for a dance right then and there. They didn't give a fuck how I look or I was going to pass out.

The club rule had a rule that we wasn't allowed to give out our phone number. You can take phone numbers from customers, but then you are supposed to go over to the bar and throw them out. Not all the dancers follow this rule. You got fired or written up.

I had a regular customers. Instead of getting lap dances, They had odd request when it came to my outfits or their weird ass fetishes. One of the dancers, who was fairly new, was trying a new move on the pole where she hooked her leg around it and stretched her body out so she was parallel to the floor. She fell on her face.

There was so much blood. As the bouncer and I were helping her off the stage, one of the customers dipped his finger in it and tasted it. Then, there was this one guy who just look for lint between my toes. That's it. Nothing really sexual except for his fetish. He would into the club around 6pm, an hour before the end of my shift so he could just to look for lint in my toes.

He would look very carefully for lint in between my toes. If a song was over, and he wasn't done looking, he'd pay for more dances. He was in the club once a week. He was my regular because the other girls didn't care for him. I got to know him and he was a really nice guy. He tipped very well, a hundred for every lint ball he find. It wasn't much. I would prefer to see him everyday instead the fucking assholes that came in.

Guys have tried to grab my legs, my hips, and my boobs. Sometimes when guys hand me money, they touch my thighs. Once a man touched my crotch, and so I yelled for help immediately and he got kicked out. The second time that happened it was from a man that had been spending tons of money on me all night. So, I told him quietly that I would give him five minutes to leave before I got him kicked out.

We always had a few that were fucking dogs. The people who made our jobs difficult, were the assholes who come in thinking that we are prostitutes and not dancers. I tried my best to stay clear them. But some days they were the best tippers. It's amazing how a tiny minority of men mentally dehumanize strippers, but we have even had our human rights and legal protections that help us out if we got in a pickle. I'm glad only a minority of customers come in with this misconception.

The most difficult part of this job is dealing with customers. It's always complicated and usually frustrating because of all the rules. Also, I can't stand rude people! I hate when customers say weird shit or make rude gestures. Another pet peeve of mine is when guys come into the club with body odor. It's repulsive. Go home and shower after work before going to the club if you stink!

I'm was a professional tease. If they tried to stick anything in me or touch me where I don't want to be touched, there are consequences. They were not entitled to force themselves onto me. The fucking rules were listed at the door in English and Spanish.

While I was dancing, I became someone else. I became this fantasy woman, and it made me feel so beautiful and desirable. The audience clapped and cheered for me. I never felt that before. Men took notice of me. Every time I hit the stage, I was fearless for those 15 minutes. Being on stage was the ultimate high. Off stage, I was just me. I heard the same thing from the other girls.

We add this awesome sexy bouncer named Axel. He was just a scary guy who was extremely intimidating, but a big teddy bear behind close doors. Axel tend to collect/payout money for couch dances and the sort. All couch/lap dance rooms had cameras in them. They were monitor in the Axel's booth and the office. Axel was supposed to keep an eye on us, making sure we were safe and that we weren't giving customers anything extra.

Axel was tall white buff biker dude. He had shoulder length bleached blonde hair. He had a goatee, which I loved the most about him. He moved here from Illinois when he was little. He looked dumb, but he was smart as hell. I had a few rounds with him outside the club.

He was ladies man. I made sure he was strapped. My pussy was disease free and wasn't about to catch anything from anyone.

As time went by, I was getting more and more regulars. As, I got into the swing of things. I went into work a couple of times only to find out that we were closing early, because we had no customers all day. Therefore I didn't have to lying about leaving early. Around six months after I began stripping, I had to find another club to work at on my off days from Illusions. Most of my regulars followed me to my next club, *Fantasy Show-bar*. Fantasy Show-bar was located in Mt. Ephraim. Fantasy Show-bar was very different from *Illusions*.

Fantasy Show-bar was a male-owned club run by a former stripper. The clientele was mainly businessmen and college students an interesting mix of big spenders and frat boys. Unlike Maxim girls, Fantasy Show-bar girls were polished and perfect in a very conventional, Jets magazine sort of way. This club was were I principally did sit-downs with clients, where someone pays for my time, and I talked to that man. My job was basically catering to the egos of the men that I was talking to. I had to pretend I was really enjoying myself, all of the time, and generate all of this positive energy.

Three things I won't leave home without was my mase, eye liner and a bottle of *Jack Daniels*. One of the rules is the dancers are not supposed to use drugs, but dancers are always doing drugs like Vicodin or Percocet. There was always two or three girls who was popping pills. They had those who was selling pills. Damn if you do and damned if you don't. My Jack is what keep me going. I always hit my bottle before I went into work.

Within the first month of me working there,

a dancer by the name Cookie had killed herself. The sound put about Cookie is that no one didn't even know she was died until closing. I went to the back to get a few things for the bar. There in the back of walk in, laid Cookie. Cookie had slit her wrist opened. God knows how long she was back there.

The police and everyone else came in to see Cookie. I was to busy focus on Cookie's arm. The cut had almost severed her left wrist, a flash of pink bone peeking through. Her right hand was curled around the handle of a utility knife. I really didn't bother me to see a dead body. I didn't even the bitch. I sat there eating my Chinese food while the others were crying. My boss pissed because he had to close the bar that night.

I worked out 3-4 days a week with a personal trainer. Between both jobs, I went through deodorant, body spray, and make-up real fast plus getting hair and nails done. Just to keep myself in *Fantasy Show-bar/ Illusion*-worthy shape. The earning potential was insane $700 to $2,000 dollars a night was pretty standard. I even started to take defensive and MMA classes.

When I was on the stage with more than half a bottle of Jack swimming around my stomach. The intense alcohol clouding the thoughts and voices that are always rattling in my head. In my suitcase, I keep the bottle close so as the whiskey high comes down I take a few more swells to put me back up where nothing matters and I numb to people around me. The downside was that I had to drive nearly four hours, round trip to work at the club. It added up, so I'm glad it's a business expense.

I would driving back home in Florence at 4 am and getting into bed at 6 am totally tweaked my sleeping schedule. Then I had to be at Illusions at 11am. It made it difficult to spend time with friends and family, but I find a way to at see my brothers and grandmom. My grandmom really didn't care about my job. She was very supportive. It didn't have to do with the fact that I gave her money when I could or when I went got her favorite platter at *Boston Market*.

WTF

I was so fucking tired getting off one job then going to another. Some days I can't remember if I was coming or going. I wanted to take a nap in the dressing room, but it was my turn to go on stage. A super old, really frail old man came up to me and hands me $100, says he wants a dance from me later. I finish my stage set and went over to his table. A younger girl was already sitting, with him.

I naturally assumed she was an escort, because the girl couldn't have been more than 18, and was wearing civilian clothes.

Old man says to me "Have you met my wife, Shirley?"

I freeze. Oh hell no! I don't care how old you are, but there was no way he was going to convince me that this girl was his wife. But then I see the rock on her hand. She's got the biggest fucking diamond ring I shrug my shoulders, shook her hand, and she immediately pulls me outside to smoke. Which was fucking cold ass balls outside. I don't smoke either, but I was making money. I really couldn't complain. I wanted to throw up. The sad part I could see him cumming. Shit was cumming out like baby powder. Fucking gross!

She pulls a flask from her bag, and offers it to me. "Do you party?", she asks.

I politely decline.

She giggles and replied, "Your lost, more for me then!" She popped a pill in her mouth. She drunk the liquid that was flask in one swallow."

I was puzzled about what she took. So I asked her.

"Oh baby girl, I took a GHB. I do this all the time" she finished.

Shit, I would have to constantly roofie myself if I was married to your husband too!" I quietly said under my breath. I had a bad feeling about this. This was going to be a long night.

She pulls me into the lap dance rooms. She started dancing with me. We're going at it for a few songs. But something was off, something was definitely not right. She started nodding her head back and forth. Turns out, this bitch was having a fucking seizure. I screamed for my manager and yelled for someone to call 911. I try to go through the steps I learned in health class. I wasn't going to leave her alone.

If she dead, at least I got paid for all those

dances. I know that was shitty thing to say. Never said I was one care that fucking much about others I didn't know. My manager ran over to help me with the girl. Finally after 5 minutes she stops shaking. I'm patting her shoulder "Shirley, do you know where you are? do you know what day it is?"

She responds to me by drooling on the floor. My manager drag her to where her husband was sitting. I was fucking naked as the day I was born, except for my 8 inch for black and red pumps. Seizure Shirley over here gets thrown into the chair.

Her fucking husband didn't give a fuck about his wife who almost fucking died. I tries pulling me into the most expensive champagne room, with a shit load of other strippers. There's was a total of 11 girls in this room, all in various states of bumping and grinding. He sat down down Porsche and Ruby. They didn't look as pretty as their names.

I try to get his attention, but his lustful gaze wasn't going to be ripped away from Mercedes and Princess. I try to crawl between legs and snake my way up without getting my face in anyone's snatch. I finally get a hold of fucking old timer. I was pissed. I could feel Tasha trying to come out. No, this time I was going to stay in control. There was way to many people around for me to allow to do what I really wanted to.

Standing over him an d began to yell at him," "Your wife almost died. You are over here getting fuck cheap feels from these skanky ass dumb bitches!"

Grandpop was pissed. He shoved the girls out of his lap, stomps down the stairs, grabs his unconscious wife and slams through the front door. I'm a little unsure as how I'm supposed to tell 11 girls that they weren't getting paid for their dances. But just then, he marched back in like nothing happened.

He walked passed me and handed each girl $500. Just to show he had control over my boss and everyone else. He handed my boss a thick ass envelope. My boss smiled and thank him. Grandpop turned around and the nerve to look at me. With grin on his face, he said," "She does this all the goddamn time. I took her to the car so she can sleep it off. I'll see you next week, Spice!"

This motherfucker was crazy. After he left, my boss pulled me into his office. He explained how I needed to mean my place. Grandpop was a regular and better be on my best better the next time he came. I didn't argue with him. Tasha and I will get him back sooner or later. I was annoyed and piss, but I went back to work.

Dancing absolutely changes you, for better and for worse, but if you're smart and lucky you will get out with some money, some good stories and only a few battle scars. I had my mix feelings about my job. Seeing the things that was going on off and on the stage was starting to get under my skin.

Chapter Fifteen

Fantasy Show-bar

Each club had it only set of some weird story or two, each week. One of the worst things I saw a dancer, Sunshine, had taken another dancer's outfit. So Sunshine does her rounds before going on stage, she walked around the bar and talked to customers so she got get some tips. Once she done her rounds, she got on the stages and started doing her routine.

Now up to this point Star had been in a Champagne Room with a customer. She had no idea what sunshine had did. She got done and shows the guy out of the room. I was seating in my booth relaxing. I watch Star making a B-line to my booth. Tonight I didn't have to dance. Which was actually a good thing. I needed a break. I was able work with Axel's in the booth. We behave, we never mix pleasure and work, when we were on the clock.

Star gets to my booth and asks for her payout for the night, so I start tallying everything up and counting out her money. Star, while waiting for me to finish my count out, starts looking around the bar and notices Sunshine, on stage with her outfit.

Star lost her fucking mind. She took off her heels and earrings. She ran to the foot of the stage and started screaming at Sunshine. The customers started chanting "Fight, fight!" Star then proceeds to hop up on stage with Sunshine. They are screaming the whole time. I called to Axel to get out here from the office. Star walked up to Sunshine and punches her square in the face.

It was funny to watch. Star went in on Sunshine. This poor girl shit herself on stage in front of the whole club. Axel was even more piss, because to pull these girls off each other.

The customers were loving it. Never a dull moment at work.

A foreign girl had just started working here. We only knew her as Lucy. Lucy was from Prague. Her barely could speak English. We didn't mess with her. Something was right with her. I knew that look very well. Lucy had red, straight hair clumsily hangs over a round. She had a very sad face, with the most gentle brown eyes. She was slender with a pouch round belly. I couldn't tell if she was pregnant but we all knew she didn't want to be there.

She was giving blow jobs in the back, because she thought that was the norm. She was used to doing extras for little pay. She got caught and had to be explained that this wasn't that country.

She was still considered dirty but she is making a killing with that experience. The girls had to give her some points in how to still do her extras, without worrying about management. She caught on quick on how to take care of management and still got to do her extras.

She was whoring around us for a few bills. We really didn't care, because they were the nasty fat fuck, that no one wanted. One day she had to dance. She was on after me. I walked over to the bar to get a quick drink.

Naturally, I ignore the girls and try to keep to myself, which I cannot help but notice something strange with outfit. I looked hard and noticed a handful of earthworms were trying to get out of her thong. WHAT THE FUCK!! This bitch was fucking nasty. My boss the fat bastard he was, was disturb what he was witnessing. He walked to the of the stage. The girl kept dancing like she didn't even care that a bunch of worms were coming out her pussy.

She spins around and comes in for another cunt swoop. My boss saw or smell, made him throw up. She laid down on the stage spread her fucking legs open. She then reached down her thong and grab the worms and throw them at my boss.

I can't take it. My eyes are starting to water. It wanted to throw up but I was trying so hard not to laugh. Edward the worse bouncer in the world, just walked in catch was going on. He looked at my boss and turned around and left.

I knew what that meant, he quit. She got up off the stage and commence to walk over my boss. She pushed him. He lost his balance and fall back on the floor. He was yelling for some one to help him. None of us dare to help him. She grabbed two knives behind the bar. She stood over my boss and speared them into his chest. Then pulled the knives down to his groin. She opened him up like a pig.

As he was screaming, blood was pouring out him. He was dying and there was nothing we could do for him. Everyone ran out the club as the police came in. The cops had their guns draw on her. They order to put the knives down. She sat on the edge of the stage, she looked the cops and in one move, she slit her throat opened. She fell back on the stage. That was the most exciting day.

For a while there, I almost forgot my hungry to kill. At the same time, while I was horrified and grossed out and disgusted by my job, I was really excited by the vast amount of money. I got addicted to that fast money and the lifestyle.

That was the last night that club was opened. Months later they knocked down the club and turned it into *Taco Bell*.

I later find out later the boss had been kidnapping and trafficking young girls. He was part of the same secret sex club/pedophile ring Miles was in. I got so catch up in working that I almost forgot about the club. It was now two years later, since Miles death.

Wow it's has been that long since I killed anyone and anything. I have been focus on getting my life straight. I went home and pulled out my yellow notebook. There was my boss's information on page 20 Jacob Carpenter.

Tasha

Taking my clothes off for money and lie. All day all, I want to do is crawl in my bed, pull the covers up over my head and sleep it away. I couldn't sleep. I sat up doing a research about the people in my yellow book. Half of the guys on my list was either in jail or living close by.

I spent hours on the internet. I was amazed I

was able to get pictures of everyone. I have seen lot of them in club. I hoped none of them me. I was a minor when Miles died. Starting today I plan to put my plan into motion. The media can't share any of my information and my name. I just hope no one puts two and two together. It was time to go to work.

I had a bad feeling about going in. It was time for me to go to work. I arrived at work and parked my car from the building. I sit in my car for a few minutes of peace and quiet before I go into my "wonderful" job. I took one last sip of my drink and exhale the bullshit, while clearing my head. I have to be on a whole different bullshit level before I start my night. I hop out the car and pop the trunk to get my suitcase out and then I hit the locks.

"Hey Spice", at the door sat the security guy Ron. He greeted me every time I come in.

"Hey Boo." I reply. I was a real flirt when was time to go to work.

I open the door and there is a small crowd already with the music blasting and the dancers doing their thing. Typical crowd for a Friday at 9 o'clock in the evening.

I went inside anyway. I walked through

the crowd, past loud groups of young men and disdainful groups of old farts, past noise flooding out of bars and groups of smokers next to doorways I remember my first time on stage, all the negative feelings came back to me hard. I should have turned back around and left.

It was time to become Spice/Josephine, my alter ego. She could handle anything, she was fearless. I love switching into Spice/Josephine, because Josephine could turn herself into anyone she wanted to be. Thank God I had a new bottle of Jack in my bag. I took half of bottle of Jack. I grabbed a Lozepam out of my tiny antique pill box and washed it down with cheap bubbly.

I was ready to go out. The clock struck 10:30 and by then I was feeling the pills and the drinks that I guzzled down. I was in the mood now to go out on the floor and take all the bullshit that comes with being a stripper. The music started and I slowly made my way onto the stage, wiggling my hips as much as I dared assuming it made me look sexy. I'd decided on sexy secretary as my first outfit so I didn't have to buy much. I was wearing a white blouse and black mini skirt over black bra, panties and stockings. I swayed a little in time to the music as I pulled the clips from my hair and shook it loose.

Slowly, I began to unbutton my blouse until it was open all the way to my skirt. Tugging it free from my waist band I was beginning to feel very uncomfortable and was hoping it was not showing. I unbuttoned the cuffs and shrugged it free and let it drop to the floor. Something just didn't right deep inside.

"C'mon girl, show us your tits" shouted someone near the front. I have to say this was not as easy as I was hoping. I was more nervous than the first time I danced. My fingers were trembling as I started to unzip my short skirt as I then let it join my blouse on the floor. I started to move around the stage again as sensuously as I could but was finding it difficult merely to put one foot in front of the other.

C'mon love we haven't got all night" shouted the old drunk man again, backed up by other shouted comments from others. I couldn't really hear what was being said. Deciding to try to settle the customers I decided to take off my bra before undoing my stockings so reached behind me to unhook it.

My fingers were trembling so much I struggled at first but then I felt it come free. I crossed my arms across my breasts before allowing the straps of my bra to fall down my arms. I slowly took my arms out one at a time till I was just left with my hands covering my breasts. It's now or never girl I told myself, just thought about my bills. With a bit of a flourish I squeezed my breasts particularly my nipples before moving my hands onto my hips.

Quite a few whistles went up from the audience, when I bared my breasts. Standing there topless before about 200 men was a mix of feelings fear and something else but I didn't know what. I decided to leave my stockings on and just lose the panties. I turned my back to the audience and slowly lowered my panties and stepped out of them. Swaying my hips slowly side to side in what I hoped was a sexy way I gradually turned around to face the audience with just my hands covering my fresh waxed stripped my girl.

As I was dancing, I scanned the room. I saw a few guys that caught my attention. I wanted to jump off the stage and kill the bastards. I wanted to so bad, but I didn't have the balls. The longer I stayed at work, the more the feelings was getting worse. Dancing on the floor for about an hour and I started relax with *Touch, Peel, and Stand by Days of New* and get in a groove. The dollars was starting to add up and it felt as if my bag had about $350 dollars. I could pretty much tell what I had by the weight of my little baggie I carried around.

I remember each person from my yellow book. One by one they were coming in. Tasha was itching to get out. We had to be careful and wise about executing each and everyone of these bastards. Something was up and I didn't like this at all.

What do you know? A very familiar face just walked in the door. Our eye locked the minute, when he came in. It was Victor came in the club so much that, he managed to befriend all the new staff. Because of that, us girls thought he was harmless. He even knew all the staff members by name. Now we had a change of hands, so a lot of workers had no idea about him.

Victor/Josephine

When, I first met Victor. He was awesome. Every Tuesday was biker night. He was this 5'8, 150-pound man. For any old guy, he was very fit. He always came in with his dusty black jeans, biker boots and wife beaters. He always smelled like *Cool Water* with the hint motor oil. He owned a garage in Pennsylvania. He always find his way do to this club, each week. He was there from 12 until closing. He was fun to be around. He would jump on the stage and dance with us. He loved picking up the girls and jumping up and down.

He some muscle over the owner. He was able to do anything, he wanted to do. They never stopped him. Even when he went behind the bar to fix himself drinks. He pay for them them, when he wanted to. There was times I would catch my boss and him talking in the back, always giving my boss a thick envelope. I wasn't stupid I knew he was paying off my boss.

Victor was one of the customers who got what he wanted when he wanted. If he didn't get what he wanted, someone had to pay for it. I did my best to stay away from him.

One day an email came from another club explaining that Victor was no longer allowed in the club and that if we saw him outside the club it would be best for us to avoid him. Victor had a dark side, we didn't know about. He was a total stalker. I don't anyone knew he was in the "club". But I'm pretty others knew the deal with him.

There was a dancer named Giselle. She was a 16 year old, medium size girl with bluest eyes. Giselle was Dublin Ireland. She had the brightest red curly long hair. She was here to visit the US, disappeared for a minute, and then all of sudden she was a stripper.

Rumor has it, that she was at a private party and was passed around like a two dollar whore. She was invited to the party by a stripper who pretend to be her friend. They beat her badly. They drugged her up and keep her for months. Victor had kidnapped and sexually assaulted her. The guy had tortured, electrocute-shocked and made to believe that she was being watched homemade rape porn of other club members who also beat and rapped her. At the beginning when Giselle would fight back., victor would punished with stun gun.

There were times, she was put in a coffin-sized box, to keep her running away. They put chains around her neck and body as well. Victor was a sadist and used Giselle as his sex slave. There were days, he would put Giselle in the box that he kept under the bed he shared with his wife. Once Victor finally broke her to be a girl. He let her out, but he was always nearby when she started working at *The Gentleman's Club* in Burlington. Victor did implant a tracking chip in her. Til this very day, we have no idea who was the stripper was that betrayed her.

I met Giselle after the incident. She came in the club looking for a job. Victor made sure she never stand at one place for to long. The look in her eyes, I could see an empty soul. She was dead inside. She got hired, but with in the first two weeks, she was showing signs that she was using. My boss fired the day we find her in the bathroom. She had a needle in her arm.

Foam was coming out of her mouth. She was overdosing. We had to make her throw up by sticking our finger down her throat. Once the paramedics came in, my boss had Sparkle clean out her locker and placed them out by the trash. She never showed up at the club. She was discovered three days later, in the Mill Dam park sitting on a bench with a needle in her arm. That was the end of the case. There was nothing else about her. It was an open and shut case.

I think it has been weeks that have went by I hadn't seen the guy. I was done my shift. Axel was to busy flirting with Sparkle. Today Axel decide to be a dick so I didn't have time to wait for him. I don't want to go to my car alone. It wasn't a really good idea, but I was too tired to wait for him. so I just headed to my car. There by car was a dozen of black and red tulips with a enveloped. I picked up the flowers.

I looked around to see if anyone was outside. I quickly opened my car trunk to put my stuff in it. Just I closed the truck, someone grabbed me from behind. I tried every defensive move to get out their grip. I was even screaming at the top of my lungs. Sky walked up to me. Now, I knew who was the stripper who helped Victor.

She grabbed my face. I looked the bitch in her eyes and spit in her face. She was piss! She covered my mouth with a cloth before you know I was out.

Being Knapp/Jada

Sky and Victor had kidnapped Sparkle as well. We believed they taken us to his house in Maryland. It was only know address that was hard for me to find. Victor liked being off the grid. We were tied up in his attic. I looked around to find ways to break from the ropes that were around my hands. Sky like a dumb bitch started screaming. I tried to shut her up but she wouldn't stop. Victor broke into the attic. He slapped me across my face. Fucking Aaliyah fucking slipped out. Bitch started freaking out. Between Aaliyah and Sky screaming, Victor was turning red.

Victor yelled at them. They won't stop, so Victor punch Aaliyah in the mouth. That quick I was back. I shut the fuck up real quick. He stood over me and said, "Y'all bitches are going to make you some money. Spice or shall I say Aaliyah Churchill. Yeah especially you. Miles told me about your sweet ass. I have been watching you since I realize who you were. Are you comfortable right now? I know you know what happened to Miles. you had him killed."

Aaliyah didn't answer him. I wanted to sat that Tasha killed him, but I wasn't about let him tortured me to get the information out of me. Our wrists and ankles chained. We were gagged. We was a little disoriented and scared.

Sky won't stop. Victor stood over and kept hitting her until she passed out. There was two dirty ass mattress in the corner of the room. There was a bathroom with no door. There was an awful smell. I can't shake. I knew what the smell was, it was a combination of urine, feces, and decomposed body.

I had no idea how long I was there. Victor and his fucking friends took turn raped Sparkle and myself. I didn't dare to fight them. Sparkle wasn't as lucky. They drugged her and beat on her. She had gotten the worse of things. They actually give us a little bit of food. I could barely fight them I was so weak.

I don't know how I was going to fight these

guy off. Depending on how well behave we were; Victor's wife would actually cooking us a big meal. Victor introduce us to his wife. Bitch had teeth no direction and color reminded of an old 70 early old woman. She looked like washed up druggy.

Sparkle barely ate because she was always in and out of concision. Sparkle was pissing off the wife each time. One day as we were seating there at the dinning table, Sparkle passed out for a few seconds.

When she woke back up, she jumped up and threw up all over the table. Victor's wife Becky was piss. She dumped boiling hot water down her back. Victor came out of his man cave. Victor beat the shit out of Sparkle until she was knocked out. He force us back in the attic. He proceed to rape her while she was unconscious.

Sparkle was getting the worse of things, because she wouldn't just shut her fucking mouth and play the good little girl. He started beating her with a chain in all of her body. He punched her with his fists. He kicked her, pulled her hair, and spit in the face. There was a day he had enough of her that he burned her with the iron.

Victor broke the sliding glass door and made Diamond was through the glass. Once she got outside, he threw her food on top of the glass and made her eat her food. Later, that night she was coughing up blood. We tried to help her but there wasn't nothing we could do. By the next morning, she was died.

Over the next few days, I was to care for Sparkle's burn, but by the end of the day her back was ripped opened, because Victor's friends came over every night to continue to rape and beat on her. They would strapped me against a beam and taped my eyes opened. They forced me to watch. When they were done with her, some of them would leave but there was always a few that would rape me as well.

The smell was getting worse. Victor decided that he was going to clean house. I had no idea what he was talking about. As watch for one of the mattress, I watched him pull out a stroller out of the closet and revealing a decomposed body. The skin hanging off of it. As Victor was cleaning the body out of the closet. He laughed how he killed his own mother and stuck her in the closet.

I was even more scared because I could see the evil in his eyes. I didn't know if I was a match for Victor. I was pretty sure that if we didn't what wanted, He was going to get rid of us. He raped us that night before he took his mother out of the room. I didn't have the answers to get free. For once Josephine was afraid to come out, but I had to force Aaliyah out. I only did this so if we make it out alive; I needed the over-drama girl to present a great case.

Each week more girls were brought to the house, just much as the trash. I watched from the window as brought in new girls. Some where put up here with us or in the bedrooms. Victor branded her with a tattoo that read property of and then were sent up here for us to care for them. These girls were from the ages of 13 and up. Some were banging for their mothers. We had to teach them to control their emotions.

As the days and weeks went by we giving

our rooms, but no without rules and cameras. We locked in with bars on the window. Two girls per room. The girl that was in my room, was a 15-year old girl who was a runaway. Therefore you know what that meant. She wasn't chained to anything, nor was drugged, no visible bruises, and she looked happy. I thought, maybe I'm missing something. If were not in the dining room or our rooms. Victor had force us to engage in prostitution turning over all the proceeds our earnings to Victor and Becky. Being forced to have sex with numerous men on a daily basis in exchange for money.

When we returned home, Becky would give us a bunch of pills and check us out to make sure we shower and didn't have any weapons/ money on us. The pills were combination of morning after pills and penicillin etc. We were not allow to go in our rooms. Victor would bound and gag us in a locked empty room until Becky came to get us one by one.

Getting Prepped

Sparkle was useless. Sparkle and the baby she was carrying were killed right in front of us. Sparkle' body bound at the hands and feet. She then was placed inside of a suitcase. They threw away like trash. We were not allow to speak about anything about Sparkle. Sparkle was reminded that could happen to us. We the other women had to touch the younger girls how to dance and to fake a smile. Heir spirit was destroyed. Any hope and dreams these girls had was ripped right out of them. Victor had his wife each day try on dancer clothes, and pamper us, especially after fucking all day with strangers and gang members. They were nice when they wanted to be. I learned whatever they wanted me to. Josephine and I didn't fight, we took our learns carefully. I did as we were told.

Sex parties can be ridiculously hot, but they can also be ridiculously awkward or uncomfortable! In this case this wasn't my idea of fun. Being force to dance and fucking a of bunch low life son of bitches. We had no choice but to participate in certain activities that you're going to want to say no to, but we already knew that no wasn't going to be a good enough. They were going forces us too.

The last night I was at the house, Becky told us about us having to go to a private party. I wasn't prepared mentally, physically, or emotionally, but I knew I had to. I needed to get away from this. I didn't what was going to happen. I knew not to piss off anyone off. I can still Tasha inside wanting to break free. She had so much rage and angry. Right now wasn't the time to let her out.

Chapter Sixteen

Private party/Jada

In order to cope, I mentally and emotionally unplugged. It took a lot of things to try to hold back all the emotions that I had about Victor and his fucking minions. I want to scream I wanted to cry I wanted to rip his fucking throat out. I didn't I kept my composure as best I could. I lost so much respect for myself and felt so dissociated from my physical body that I began having suicidal thoughts, but I knew that was the feelings I was getting from Josephine. It was very rare that Josephine felt that way. I knew

I had to step in. Tonight I was putting on my custom made two piece school girl outfit.

Victor pulled the truck up to the front door. Wife opened the door to let us out. We all stepped out of the trunk and lined up to go inside. Becky had us a duffel bag full of baby wipes, condoms, high-heel stilettos and skimpy dresses/customers.

We walked up to the front door of this terrace house in a leafy, conservative suburb in Millville. I felt a mixture of terror and curiosity. The house's exterior couldn't have been further from what I imagined was happening inside. I was surprised to be greeted by two biker dudes, who were friendly.

I was shock when one of them shook my hand in a very businesslike manner. I knew they were being fake. I continue to walk through the house. I recognize "family man" in the photos. I laughed at the family photos lining the hallway wall. The so called family man was a local defensive lawyer who seemed to always winning his cases of the people he represent which was all bad people.

The guys form a big circle, with one of members in the center sitting on an arm-less chair. There was all ages range from early twenties to mid-forties and making things even more awkward. There was no need for small talk. I was ignoring the dirty little elephant in the room until who was drunk and making the most noise from his chair. Bitch was to fat to see his dick even if he tried.

The younger girls was pulled out the line. They were taking down a different hallway. About 30 of men with bags and camera followed behind. They would later join us in the living room. Some were so drugged up they couldn't stand. Some of the guys noticed how vulnerable they were. They pick the girls up and throw them over their shoulders. They would grab a few of their friends, so they could gang rape the girls.

We, the older ones, started off in costumes anything from French maids to nurses and doctors to cops. I forced to dance seductively for the fat bastard sitting in the chair for about 15 minutes, showing some skin, putting our hands on his shoulders, straddling his legs, grinding his crotch with our butts, pinching his nipples. Eventually, we take off his shirt.

Next came the bondage aspect of the show. I laid on the asshole on the floor on his tummy and blindfold him. First I teased him by running feathers or ice cubes down his back, and then I started spanking and whipping him.

The bondage part takes a good 30 minutes, because after we do the groom, we do each of the groomsmen separately. The guys watching loved the bondage play. They screamed loud and yell things like "Hit him harder!".

When the bondage part was finished, our tops come off and we get down to just our G-strings, stockings, and high heels. Then another dancer pulled out some whipped cream and strawberries. I lie down on the dining room table. She puts whipped cream on my nipples and a strawberry dipped in whipped cream between my breast. Then, she slowly ate every bit of whipped cream and strawberries off me. When it's gone, the guys took turns eating a dipped strawberry off my chest, using only their mouths. One of the assholes, was fucking extra by sucking super hard on my nipple. I wanted to slit everyone's throats. I was waiting on the perfect time to let Tasha. We were going to kill everyone and get the fuck out of here.

April D. Campbell

A few of the guys came over to eat strawberries off of me, another dancer dripped candle wax onto my nipples. Then it's break time. I slipped my g-string and my bra. For the next 20 minutes, my friend and I socialize with the men at the party. Deep inside I could hear Tasha. I an down the hallway were the other girls were. I slipped into the bathroom. In the bathroom I could one of the guys talking to a crying girl. If you don't do as you are told, I'm going to send this video of you in compromising positions to your families. Then when your baby sister becomes of age. I am going to kidnap her and make her do the things you should have done. You will be die and there wasn't you can do about it.

That motherfucker was sick. She bang and did as she was told to. All I could do was shake my head. I went through the medicine cabinets I find a shitload of pills. There was eight full bottles Desyrel, Silenor, and Morphine sulfate. I was able to rip the lining in my bra and dump as many pills as I could. I was able to go into the kitchen, I tapped into my waitress skills.

I had to do it quick and hoping no one had seen me. I opened as many beers I could. I then dropped as many pills in all the beers until I had no more. I took I was caught when Victor came into the room and grabbed my arm. I keep my cool. Victor looked me up and down and then grabbed the beer. He finished it in one swallow. I had served every guy a beer. Sky was ready to come out and play. She also kept a close eye on most of us, especially the younger girls. A lot of guys are very entertained by conversing with us about day-to-day stuff as we're standing there topless with drinks in our hands.

After a quick break, a young drunk of his fucking mind came up to helps us get naked. Sometimes I make him take off my panties with his teeth One of the nasty ass bastards came over and began to suck my toes. I hate fucking feet. I also knew that if I didn't let these bastards, only God knows what Victor would do if he got wind of me not playing nice.

Then another dancer and me started french kissing me. I wanted to threw up. Her breath reek of cigarettes and beer. They love it! It's so erotic to them. Some guys moan. Some guys scream. They ask us to do it again. And again, and again. Therefore, we kiss, and we kiss, and then we went into hardcore girl-on-girl action:

kissing, sucking, licking. She sucks my toes and nibbles on my legs and inner thighs. There's lots of neck biting, lots of nipple play, and ultimately, oral sex.

While this is going on, the guys are yelling things like "Woo hoo! Oh my God! "Holy shit, I can't believe I'm seeing this! "This is better than porn!"

That fucker came over to us and snatched me off the stage. He took me into the back room and did what he wanted to do. When he was done with the physical and sexual abuse, he got dress. Just then he got a phone call and rushed out of the room. I never seen the guy for the rest of the night. I cleaned myself up and put on another outfits. I went back out to the crowd of me. I stood in the corner scared. I didn't know what to do. I had to calm down. I started tugging my ear. I walked into the kitchen and grabbed a bottle of ice cold water. I gathered myself to go back out to perform before Victor or Becky realize I wasn't working.

All of a sudden, right in the middle of our show, a guy pulled out his penis and started playing with himself. In front of everybody! His father walked up to him and said, "Son, are you sure you want to be doing this?" The kid slurred "Leave me alone" and just kept going. He eventually passed out cold with it in his hand. One by one the crowd started to quick down everyone was getting sleepy. I was even surprised that Sky, Victor, and Becky were a sleep. Fuck, even some of the dancers were falling asleep. I guess every man for themselves.

Some fun/Tasha

I was gone the minute I was in charged. I went from room to room cutting and shooting everyone I came across. I couldn't even tell you who was dead or alive. I did what I had to do as each man and girl dropped in their paths. Some fought back. They didn't win, I was gone. I didn't care who I was hurting and killing. I can't even tell you, if I killed Victor and the reason. When I started in the living were Victor and the rest were. I stood in the middle of a hot mess. Blood and guts were every where. I took a deep breath.

I had blood and people's guts all over me. No

one was safe that day. It was biggest massacre and first in the history of New Jersey. I was bleeding everywhere. The adrenaline was running through my veins. All I could see was red because the blood that was dripping from hair and face.

Escape

Fight over flight start to kick in. I wasn't sure if I got everyone but I needed to get away. I never seen such terror in my life. I ran for the front door. There on the coat hooks in the corner of the room hanging there was the girl who shared a room with. I can't even tell you if I did this. I grabbed a coat and put it on. I ran out down a flight of stairs in front of the house. I didn't dare to look back.

I running for miles. I can't feel my legs anymore. Everything was starting to become numb. Maybe I should lay down, yes that would be best. I needed to save my energy, there's no use in wasting it like this. If I lay down on the side of the road. I will make it out of here alive, I'm sure of it.

Somebody will find me soon, so I'll just lay down for now. I'm was going to die. Shame it's wasn't like in the movies. I have yet to see flashes of my life as I slowly regain my strength. No, I refuse. I will not die today. I was strong. I am strong. I will make it out of this. Somebody will find me and if not and I wasn't going to just lay there waiting to find out. I was so cold. I didn't notice it before, but my body started to shiver. It wasn't cold out here My body feels numb, but I still feel cold. It was starting to get dark, when I finally seen a house with all the light on inside.

I finally made my way to the house. I bang on the door. I scared the hell out of everybody that was there. A lady came out and wrapped a blanket around me, as another one called the police.

As, I sat there and waited with the cop and the ambulance. I had to show them where this party was and where did I come from. They promise to keep me safe. I couldn't remember the address, but I remember how to get there. I stayed in the police car when they arrived. I felt a relief. At the same time I I was hoping that everyone was dead.

I've put my head back in the seat. I was all bandage up. There was a puddle of my own blood that was leaking from my arm. I guess this is the end of the line for me. Just I took a deep breath, I felt this piercing pain in my stomach and in my head.

I woke to find me in the hospitals, with tubes everywhere. My body is one big mess, I can feel it. I had no idea what happened. The doctors came in to explained that I survive from 6 gunshots wounds to my body and two to my head. I was in a coma for five weeks.

I couldn't remember everything. It was brought to my attention that I was missing for three months. It was my grandmom who filed a missing person report. I had to stay in the hospital for a few more days. I then transfer to rehab, because I needed a couple weeks to get back on my feet. I had protection 24/7. The police came up to visit me everything they needed answers. My grandma and my cousin cared for me. I didn't care for my cousin but I was happy to see my grandmom and brothers.

I laid in the rehab. I remember hearing that some of the victims had dead but there were a few that survived the brutal attack. The story was all over the news. My name was never release. The courts and police kept my ID and information linking out. They were able to close the case without me being in front everyone. Everything came to light. There was some big names that was killed in that house. There was a bunch of nobody's but there was police, judges, doctors that was killed at the party. The case became a national scandal, impacted by issues of race, politics and class. Unfortunately, the horrific memories may very well last a life time but I can only remember bits and pieces.

Chapter Seventeen

Recovering

I didn't know why Phyllisa want me to move back in with her. My cousin was annoying. I was able to go back to my place. People kept stopping by my place to see if I was okay and to see how I was recovering from the kidnapping. I plead the fifth in all areas. I was in my house plotting how to seek revenge and how to get after the rest of the guys that was part of the club. I searched high and low for my yellow book. I couldn't remember anyone and their names.

I quit working as a stripper. The need to kill people was under control. I wanted to clean the earth of this filth pedophiles human trafficking rapist sexual sick bastards. I had no problem hurting people. I went back to school to do my preparations for graduation. I worked at average jobs. I did my best to maintain my thirst to kill and seek revenge on people who deserve it.

I went back to my high school to practice for my upcoming graduation. I decide to show back up giving my grandma the ultimate dream, which was to see me walk down with my class. The school that I love so much but at the same time, I hated it, because so many people were so fucking fake.

It was nice to see a lot of my friends and to be able to graduate with them but they were surprise to see me there. They all ask what happened to me. I didn't share much with them. I don't know if they would consider me a friend or enemy it's funny. I wore a nice white satin dress under my white gown. I took my diploma with pride and walked down off the looking at my grandma and a new man in my life.

Dr. Gil Howard/ Finally Visit

"Now you know, everything about me."

"Wow! Tasha, you been through a lot."

"Who is Tasha?"

"I'm sorry, I mixed your name up with another person. Please forgive me. I know you been seeing me for weeks. I have so many cases. Refresh my memory please. What is your name?'

"It's okay! My name is Aaliyah. Is there anyway we go get something to drink or to eat?"

"Sure, I have a few things to do before I leave. Why don't we finish your session, while you are here?"

"I really don't feel comfortable and need to relax."

"How's this we can meet up at a local bar by Motel Inn on Rt 38 in Lumberton."

"Do remember every person from the party?"

"No, I haven't, why you asked?"

"I was just wondering."

I headed over the bar and got the best seats. I avoided eye contact with any one and all the cameras. We were so fucked up that Gil wanted to get a room. I stayed in bar until he returned. Before going to the room, I grabbed my bag from the car. We giggled and walked to the back of the hotel to room 187.

"It got us a double queen beds."

"Awesome!"

Gil walked in first and I followed him in. As soon as the door closed behind me and locked in. I closed the curtains. Gil was falling all over the place. He landed on bed closet to the bathroom. I took my bag and went the bathroom. I freshen up. I prepared a syringe and slipped in the back of my bra strap.

As, he laid there handcuffed to bed. He was so fucked. I stuck a syringe in his neck. "Ouch.... what the fuck was that?"

"I just gave you something help you relax."

As, my "special" was slowly kicking in. "Oh wow, whatever you gave feels good but I can't feel my legs." His words started to slur. He tried to talk, but nothing was coming out. I watched as showed panic in his eyes. He couldn't talk or move.

"It's okay. I stood at the end edge of the bed. I have an confession. I have been watching you for years. I had to wait until I get to you. I pulled off my wig. I popped out my contacts to reveal my true color. I wiped my make off. You asked me do I remember people from my yellow notebook. I do! I remembered everything.

"You were the bastard that was screaming at the top of your mouth and then you snatched me. You acted like you cared. Then punch me in my face. I fell to the floor. Then you acted as if you cared. You picked me off the floor. Then punched me again. You knew I wasn't able to fight back. You threw me onto the bed and raped me raw and hard. I can still feel pain once in a while in my eye socket. who beat and cut me up. I couldn't do anything. You stood over my body and laugh and spit on me."

I learned years later that the house I went to for that private party was owned by your brother Jebediah Howard. Ten years later, I took the time to find everyone who was part of that party. One by one I killed everyone of them. You are the last one!

There was terror in his eyes. I got dress and put on some protective gear. I continued to talk to him. I explained that I didn't like hurting kids. But I made exception in this situation. The baby sitter who has been watching son for the longest, was the daughter of one the strippers y'all had fun with at that party. She was unconscious and laying up in the hospitals in a coma on life support. Her parents didn't believe in abortion. They made the doctors kept her until it was time for to give birth. They cut the baby out and let their pass away 3 days later.

She was able this morning to gain full custody and name change of your son. She is disappearing with him as we seat here. Memories of son will be wiped from his memory. The baby sitter was ordered to care for your son over the last year. She has no idea about me. She was giving all the information about her mother and you a year ago. Yes it was me. Nothing can link it to me. Your family is dead.

My name is Jada. I cared for Aaliyah and the others. I showed up more after Aaliyah's brothers were forced out. I kept a lot of the information about me. Over the years I learned a lot from Josephine and Tasha. I am the more mature version of them. My heart is cold and black. I personally don't give fuck about you or anyone else. My circle was and has been small. I like it like that.

I was time for me to go to work. I slowly sliced him open with such great precision *Mozart's Lacrimosa* played in background. I had the perfect flaying knives that I find in an antique store. I clean and sharpen to perfections. This was the perfect time to use them. I had flay him. I was able peel back his skin layer by layer and revealing every inch of him. I hooked him to the ceiling by fish hooks. I pretended to be him and called the front desk telling them to charge my credit card for me to extend my stay for a week at the hotel and please don't have people come to my room.

He was still alive as I got nake and slipped on his skin. I danced to the violins. I was behind sick and twisted. I was evil and I was losing all empathy towards people. When the song was over, I draped the skin on the dresser in front of him. I took his boxers and placed them in his mouth. I then duct taped his mouth shut. The tears were pouring down his face. I really didn't care I cleaned all my tools and myself.

Once I was done with everything. I sat down and watched Gil for an hour. I gathered my stuff, turned on the TV, and blasted the air condition on. I took one last look at him. I put the "Don't Disturb" sign on the door. I slipped into the night like a ghost. Not every the people at the hotel seen me.

About two weeks, on the news, there he was Dr. Gil Howard. They discovered his body a week later, when it was time for him to check out. Once again the police had no clue and no evidence who killed him. His parents filed a missing person report on Gil and his missing son. They were never going to find his son. His was a ghost. They find DNA besides his in the room. They did test it, but when it was mixed with some kind of chemical which made it hard for them to get a positive test on who it might be.

Double life

How do you go back to being normal after making upwards of $2,000 a day? I now live a double life. I've crossed over to the dark side. There is no help for me now. I used to be so nice and kind. I changed up how I killed people. Each new kill became just excited as my first but better.

Now my stage involves balancing bills and caring for family. Don't get me wrong! I love that I have a family, but I can't help but to think about all the things I could have or where I could be now if I didn't have my new family and life.

There are times I do seat back and reflect on the past. Especially all the money I had then. I can't happy, but to think about how I got here. Don't get me wrong I love my new life. I just know I had to be careful. I guess I will never know but the life I live and for those who have a problem with the way I lived my life., sit back and think about what the fuck have you do lately! I know I wasn't perfect but hell if I was asked to do it again……..I would!

Upon returning to "normal" society, however, it became necessary for me to adopt a more mainstream schedule. Being at work at 9am is crappy, but not nearly as crappy as being at work at 7am. I love coming home to my three boys. When I was out with my kids I put in my contacts and always kept my hair on point. Never revealing the truth of how revealing look under it.

If you are wondering how Scott is doing. Well, I ended up catching him. He was fucking a bitch from my old job. She didn't recognize me. At gun point I made Scott tie her drown in a chair and gagged her. Once he was done, I did the same thing to him. I was always prepared to kill and hurt others. I drugged them both so they couldn't fight back. They both couldn't make any noise. I made Scott watched me as I scraped the bitch and performed lobotomy on her and Scott.

I gave them sleeping pills and placed them in the bed together. Once again I cleaned up and I actually left them alive. Three days, later I got a call from the hospital to come and talk about Scott. Scott was put in a mental institute. Scott was now a mute and vacant-minded. The girl was find in the bathroom dead. She had committed suicide.

I went on my life. I tried to be a social bug from time to time. When people ask you "What did you do before this?" I tend to come up with some creative answers depending on the company I kept and what I would imagine their reaction would be. Not everyone is so open and accepting of dancers, as we well know. I am pretty sure if they knew I was a killer. Would they still want to get to know me?

I love and live for the killer. I may not have easy as I use to when I was a killer, but a woman with find a way to take her wrath out in so many way. Know that I understand who I am what makes you think you may not be the next one on my victims list.

I kill for justice and for the pleasure. I am mine worst enemies and best friend all rolled in one. The twisted game was the sexual thrill I get from striking terror. I don't think people realize who they are fucking with anymore. I'm NOT that simple bitch that is just going to take people's shit. I walk alone, well a least that is what you see.

I guess now you can just say I have learned to put myself in situations to allow myself to feast on my desires to kill. To bad you can't join my friends and me. We are having a pig roast. Underneath the slab of concrete, lays the bodies of those I have killed. My fiancee build a gorgeous fire pit in the center. I will save the details about my family and fiancee for another time.

It's believe that the most damage is the one people would have to worry about. Because we really don't have much to live for. I would be label a serial killer. I need have a *signature* which was actually more important, but at the same time, I didn't people to realize it was the same person. My scars remind me what I have been through' but they don't dictate where I'm going. Be careful who piss off. I am one bat shit crazy savage bitch. I have no problem seeking revenge..........HAHAHAHA!

Connecting with April

Find April on social media by visiting
Facebook @AuthorAprilCampbell,
Twitter @ Apriltazi on Instagram @
authoraprilcampbell, and you can email
April at Apriltazi@gmail.com.

Printed in the United States
By Bookmasters